AF560818

Get Over It

Books by Liisa Kyle

You Can Change Your Life: A Workbook to Become the Person You Want to Be

Self-Worth Essentials: A Workbook to Understand Yourself, Accept Yourself, Like Yourself, Respect Yourself, Be Confident, Enjoy Yourself, and Love Yourself

Life Levers: Make Small Changes to Create Big Improvements in Your Life

You Can Get It Done: Choose What to Do, Plan, Start, Stay on Track, Overcome Obstacles, and Finish

Coping in Times of Crisis: Ways to Handle Uncertainty and Navigate the Unknown Future

Overcoming Perfectionism: Solutions for Perfectionists

Overcoming Emotional Eating: Coach Yourself to Manage Cravings, Eat Mindfully, and Foster a Healthy Relationship with Food

Making the Most of 2025: A Workbook

Be More Creative: 101 Activities to Unleash and Grow Your Creativity

Making the Most of Your Retirement: Ways to Foster Health, Happiness & Fulfillment at Any Age

Know Yourself Better: Self-Discovery Questions and Activities

Coach Yourself: Self-Coaching Questions and Activities for Self-Discovery and Personal Growth

40 Ways to Enjoy Turning Forty: Make the Most of Your Milestone Birthday to Have the Best Year Ever

50 Ways to Enjoy Turning Fifty: Make the Most of Your Milestone Birthday to Have the Best Year Ever

Making the Most of Your Milestone Birthday: 52 Ways to Have the Best Year Ever

Coping with the Virus Crisis: Ways to Handle Uncertainty and Navigate the New Normal

Get Over It

OVERCOME REGRET,
DISAPPOINTMENTS,
AND PAST MISTAKES

Liisa Kyle, PhD

ALEPH BOOK COMPANY
An independent publishing firm
promoted by ***Rupa Publications India***

Published in 2022 by Shimmer Press

Published in India in 2024
by Aleph Book Company
7/16 Ansari Road, Daryaganj
New Delhi 110 002

Cover illustration: Shutterstock/Mary Long

ISBN: 978-81-970811-5-6

1 3 5 7 9 10 8 6 4 2

Printed in India

Contents

CHAPTER 1

What Is Holding You Back?

Are you dwelling on past regrets, disappointments, and perceived mistakes?

Do you berate yourself for things you did? This might include:

- Decisions you made
- Actions you took
- Things you said
- Opportunities you attempted
- Your perceived "mistakes"

Or maybe you are kicking yourself for things you didn't do, such as:

- Paths you didn't follow
- Missed opportunities
- Things you didn't say when you had the chance

Are you punishing yourself with "Coulda Woulda Shoulda" thinking? Do you fret about how things might have turned out differently *if only* you would have made a different decision or taken an alternative course of action?

You are not alone. Every person makes mistakes. Everyone experiences regrets and disappointments in life.

What differs is how people deal with them. Some people acknowledge what happened, learn what they can from it, and move on. Some of us have a harder time letting go. We cling to our perceived failures and let them fester.

Look at how the people you know handle their regrets. Of those, who would you like to emulate? Uncle Biff who has never gotten over missing a catch in the big varsity game—or Aunt Buffy who made and lost a million bucks and laughed her way through the process of making her subsequent million?

You could seek inspiration in celebrities, too. For example, consider some of the people who **lost** when they competed on *Star Search* (an influential American television show): Aaliyah, Christina Aguilera, Beyoncé, Drew Carey, Alanis Morissette, Rosie O'Donnell, LeAnn Rimes, Britney Spears, Justin Timberlake, and Usher. In fact, pretty much any celebrity you know had to overcome some disappointments, regrets, and "mistakes" to become successful.

Al Pacino turned down not only the role of Hans Solo in *Star Wars* but also the lead male role in *Pretty Woman* that was played by Richard Gere. A less secure person might drown in the regret of missing out on not one but two major hits...yet Pacino didn't let these events cloud his considerable career.

ACTIVITY

Think of the people you know. How have they responded to regrets or disappointments they faced? Who are good role models for you?

Consider this story: Bethany Hamilton was a promising competitive surfer until she was horribly mutilated by a 4.3-metre-long tiger shark. She lost her left arm and sixty percent of her blood in the attack. She almost died en route to the hospital. At only thirteen years old, she was now an amputee.

Put yourself in Bethany's place for a moment. Imagine that you are thirteen years old and lose your left arm in a vicious shark attack. What would you do? How would you feel about going back into the ocean? How would you have handled the loss of your arm—at age thirteen?

Under those circumstances, it would be very easy to become depressed and self-conscious. To avoid the sea at all costs. To regret going surfing in the first place. *"How could I have been so careless and stupid?"* To expect to live a sad and limited life.

Here's a different version of the same story: when she lost her left arm in a life-threatening shark attack, thirteen-year-old Bethany Hamilton displayed amazing courage and strength in clinging onto life as she was rushed to the hospital. Her passion for surfing remained strong and unwavering. Now an amputee, she taught herself to surf with only one arm and resumed competitive surfing just twenty-six days after the attack. Today, at age thirty-four, she is a professional surfer, writer, philanthropist, and happily married mother of four. Her story has inspired millions to face and overcome their own challenges.

A couple of points here: no matter what happens to you, you have a choice as to how you want to live your life, going forward. Bethany could have given up. (I know I probably would have, under the circumstances.) She didn't. She turned this horrible incident into an opportunity to pursue a life path that has been wonderful for her.

Second, you have a choice about how long you will let what happened affect you. In Bethany's case, it was less than a month. What about you?

When negative events happen, it is natural to feel sad, upset, or angry. Go ahead and mourn. Punch a pillow. Have a brief pity party. But put a time limit on your reaction. The longer you stew or fret, the heftier the toll you are putting on yourself and those around you.

Regret keeps you stuck in the past and siphons off your hopes for your future. It can swell to excess. If you feel like you have "ruined everything", that hopelessness will blind you to what is possible *now*. You will be missing the new opportunities that are arising around you all the time. Helen Keller said, "When one door closes, another opens. But often we look so long so regretfully upon the closed door that we fail to see the one that has opened for us."

If you are spending too much time and energy thinking about the past—berating yourself for what did or didn't happen—you are squelching your present contentment and wasting energy you could be spending on activities that will enhance your future. And let's be candid—how pleasant are you to be around when you are bemoaning your regrets? Your burdens might be spilling onto people you care about.

If past events are affecting your life today—or hindering your future—you need to *get over it.*

Feel that tightness in your neck and shoulders? Hear that nagging, negative voice in your head? Imagine the relief if that was gone. Consider how much better you would feel if you would get over what happened and move on with your life.

◆

THE SOLUTION

There are proven, practical actions you can take to overcome your regrets and disappointments. You **can** *get over it.*

I'm a PhD in psychology, a life coach, and author of two dozen self-help books. I've spent the past twenty years helping people overcome regrets, disappointments, "mistakes", and missed opportunities. I've devised tools, techniques, and remedies that work. I've written this book to help you:

- Identify what burdens from the past are holding you back
- Work through what is bothering you
- Let it go and move on, and,
- Prepare yourself to deal with future experiences more effectively

Note that these techniques are designed for people having trouble letting go of regrets, disappointments, and perceived "mistakes." If you are seeking to get over a more severe trauma in your past, (for example, if you are the victim of violence or are experiencing PTSD), this book will be insufficient to meet your needs. Instead, please contact a qualified professional for clinical help. If you don't know where to start, ask your doctor.

HOW TO GET THE MOST OUT OF THIS BOOK

Begin by taking stock of what past regrets, disappointments, and mistakes are affecting you today (Chapter 2).

Next, give some attention to shifting your focus from the past to the present (Chapter 3). This helps put your past regrets and disappointments in perspective and will give you some tools and techniques to better deal with them.

Next, I recommend you take whatever regret or disappointment is foremost in your mind and work through these proven steps:

- Examine what happened (Chapter 4)
- Seek silver linings (Chapter 5)

- Tell a different story (Chapter 6)
- Forgive yourself and others (Chapter 7)
- Take action (Chapter 8), and,
- Let it go (Chapter 9)

Once you have worked through your biggest burden, you might wish to repeat the process with other regrets or disappointments you still carry. Take your time. Give each event the attention it requires. Pace yourself gently.

Each chapter features proven techniques and practical tools. Work through the contents at a pace that is comfortable and engaging for you.

You will get more out of this book if you participate. If the activity involves answering questions, it is more powerful if you actually write (or type) them out.

As you work through the activities, respond as quickly as possible, writing down as many ideas and answers as you can generate in short order. Be candid. There are no wrong answers. By writing your responses, you will elicit deeper insights and you will generate more ideas (including some surprises).

Once you begin jotting down your responses, you will notice that new insights will emerge faster and more clearly than if you simply scan the questions and assume you know how you'll respond.

It is likely that new ideas will occur to you after you complete an activity. Feel free to go back and capture whatever new insights emerge.

After you have processed some past burdens, turn to Chapter 10 to pause and consider how you would like to operate, moving forward. How can you treat yourself well? How can you utilize your strengths? What path do you choose now, at this point in your life? How can you manage your expectations? How can you deal more effectively with any future regrets or disappointments?

When you are ready to begin, turn to the next chapter.

CHAPTER 2

What Past Regrets, Disappointments, and Mistakes Are Affecting You Today?

Why are you reading this book? What experiences in your past are still bothering you?

Begin by making a list. Either write them down on paper or type them into a digital file. You will be using this list in different activities in this book, so please pause now to do the following activity:

ACTIVITY

1. What burdens from your past are you carrying today? List them. Consider:
   - Regrets
   - Disappointments
   - Perceived "mistakes"
   - Things you've done or said
   - Things you didn't do or didn't say
   - Choices or decisions you made
   - Things that happened
   - Things that didn't happen
   - Things that didn't happen the way you wanted
2. Circle or highlight the item on your list that bothers you the most.

HOW ARE THESE BURDENS AFFECTING YOU TODAY?

Consider your past regrets and disappointments. How are they affecting you today? What have you noticed? To what extent do they affect your personal life? Your work life? Your social life?

ACTIVITY

Choose one item from your answers to the second question in the preceding activity. How is this affecting your current life? Consider:

- Your thoughts
- Your beliefs
- Your decision making
- Your emotions (anger, sadness, hope, etc.)
- Your openness (to people, to experiences)
- Your level of stress
- The actions you take
- The actions you avoid

When we carry burdens from the past, we are likely incurring costs of doing so. You are probably aware of some of them. You might be unaware of others.

These costs are often disguised or hidden. Events in our past can pull invisible strings in our current lives. They might show up as a subtle shying away of someone or something—or a studious avoidance of a particular place, project, or person.

To begin to *get over* your past regrets, disappointments, and mistakes, it is helpful to pause and assess exactly what these burdens are costing you today. Are you experiencing any of the following possible prices of regret?

POSSIBLE PRICES OF REGRET

1. Wasted Time, Attention, and Energy

You can't change the past, so any time you spend dwelling on it is squandered. Period. Every minute you spend thinking about past events are stealing attention from your current situation and the people around you.

Every bit of effort you put into your past burden is siphoned from energy you could be putting into more pleasant, productive activities.

Jane was a high flyer accustomed to succeeding. When she was passed over for a promotion that went to someone less qualified, Jane found herself daydreaming about revenge fantasies for all involved. "I lost a few months just seething about what happened," she says. "What a waste. It would have been better to spend that time networking and putting out feelers for other job opportunities."

2. The Emotional Expense

Consider any emotions you expend on past events such as grief, sadness, remorse, frustration, anger. What is the toll on you, mentally and physically, to dwell in these feelings?

Jane felt awful. She was very angry and that was stressful to bear. She could feel it in her neck and shoulders every day.

3. It Creates a "Victim Mentality"

Are you blaming yourself or others for what happened? If so, you might be fostering a "victim mentality" that is unpleasant and often painful. It damages you and whatever you're doing.

In Jane's case, she blamed her boss and the person who took the position she believed was her due. She felt betrayed. All her earlier work suddenly felt spoiled—as if she'd toiled so hard for nothing. She wondered if she was the victim of misogyny or office politics. She lost all trust in all her coworkers because it felt that they had conspired against her, either tacitly or overtly.

4. It Harms Your Health

At a biochemical level, regret can throw off your hormone balance and disrupt your immune system.

The bigger the burdens of the past you carry today, the more stress you are putting on yourself, mentally and physically. Stress affects every single bodily system. The more you cling to the past, the more you are jeopardizing your current physical well-being. After a month of grumbling about the promotion she didn't get, Jane started experiencing painful back spasms that she hadn't had before.

5. It Devalues What You Have Now

No matter what you have experienced in the past, there are things to savor in your current life. The more you are focused on the past, the more you are neglecting the present...and missing opportunities to appreciate and enjoy things now.

Jane did not have the position she desired but she did have a good job. She had a regular paycheck and benefits. She also had a home and a husband and many other reasons to be grateful. For a time, however, she was blind to everything but her deep disappointment.

6. It Makes You More Negative

The more you beat yourself up for what you did or didn't do in the past, and the more you kvetch about what might have been, the more negative you are being in the here and now—and the more pessimistic you are about the future.

You probably know from your own experience that whatever you give out, you get back. The more negative thoughts you think, the more negative thoughts you foster. The more negative energy you put out, the more negative experiences you attract to yourself. This sets up a vicious circle of self-fulfilling doom.

When she lost the promotion, Jane lost her good cheer. She was sullen and quick to shoot down other people's ideas. Her colleagues started to give her a wide berth.

7. It Damages Your Relationships

Do you enjoy listening to others bemoan the past? No one else does either. The more you express your regrets and disappointments to others, the less pleasant you are to be around. You are bringing other people down and jeopardizing your relationships.

It is especially frustrating for people who care about you. They see that you are in pain and are helpless to make you feel better. The more you dwell on things no one can change, the worse you are making your loved ones feel.

Jane's husband was no exception. As the months wore on, he found it more difficult to be patient and supportive as Jane repeated her litany of the injustice she had suffered. "There is nothing I can do or say that make her feel any better. It's unbearably frustrating."

8. It Can Keep You Stuck

To the extent you are dwelling on past regrets and disappointments, you are not moving forward. You might find yourself stuck for a long period of time.

It fosters a false belief that because bad things have happened in the past, bad things will continue to happen to you, no matter what you do. It creates a sense of hopelessness and an expectation of inevitable, unavoidable misfortune.

Jane wallowed for months. She went through the motions at work. What was the point of working hard? Nothing she did would be properly recognized or rewarded.

9. It May Cause You to Avoid People, Places, Things, Activities, and Opportunities

If you have not gotten over something, you may be cutting people, places, or activities out of your life unnecessarily. Have you given up an activity you loved because of a past regret or disappointment? Have you had the experience of disliking someone when you first meet them because they resemble someone from your past?

It can also make you fearful to take risks, lest you fail or incur more regrets or disappointments. But what happened in the past does not necessarily predict what will happen in the future. If you avoid trying something again or trying something new, you are missing out of new opportunities.

Jane was hesitant to network because of the trust she'd lost in her colleagues. As she met new people, she was instantly repelled by anyone who reminded her of her boss. This complicated and slowed her search for another job. It took a long time for her to find a place in an organization where she felt safe and appreciated.

KEY QUESTIONS

Consider the item you chose in the activity on p. 9.

- How much time, attention, and energy have you spent thinking about this?
- When you dwell on this, what feelings do you experience?

- What is the toll of these emotions on you?
- To what extent do you see yourself as a victim? How does this manifest? How does it affect your thoughts and your actions?
- When you think about this, are you aware of any tension in your body? What is the impact on your physical well-being?
- When you think about this, how does it affect how you perceive your current life?
- What is the impact of this on the people around you? (If you're unsure, ask them.)
- To what extent do you feel stuck?
- What people, places, thing, or activities are you avoiding, as a result of this past experience?
- What opportunities might you be missing, as a result of this past experience?

Despite these costs, many of us dwell on our regrets and disappointments ...so we must be getting something out of doing so. If we weren't getting some benefits, we would have stopped long ago.

Consider if any of the following are true for you:

POSSIBLE BENEFITS OF REGRET

1. It's Easy

If you are dwelling on past events, you are probably reliving them the same way, over and over. As you do, you are wearing a groove of "Coulda Woulda Shoulda" thinking that has become a habit. It is easier to keep doing what you've been doing than to disrupt that pattern.

It would take effort and energy to challenge your beliefs about what happened, to learn from your experience, or to reframe how you think about it.

2. You Can Get Attention and Sympathy from Others

The first time you tell someone about a past regret or disappointment, they are likely to be attentive, sympathetic, and supportive. They may empathize. They may commiserate with you and validate your experience. You may feel closer to them. That can feel good. That can motivate you to repeat your stories.

The more you tell others about past regrets or disappointments, the more attention and sympathy you may gain. That can be gratifying and tough to give up.

Some people might keep you in a "victim" role, consciously or subconsciously. They might enjoy feeling stronger or "better" or believing that they would have done things differently. They might want to steer you in a new direction "for your own good". They might reinforce your fears about how awful and damaging this event was. *"Poor you, of course you should give up that silly notion of trying to write a novel. Be practical. Get a nice, safe job in accounting. Earn a pension."*

3. It Can Be a Backhanded Way of Bragging about Your Abilities

"I was rejected by Spielberg!"; "The editor loved my book but the bean counters on the editorial committee nixed the deal."; "I could have been a contender!"

Sentiments like this let you and others see that you have been very, very close to greatness, once upon a time. It can be comfortable to dwell in this space of "what might have been" and let yourself off the hook for any future endeavors.

4. You Might Be Right

It could be that you are 100 per cent correct in your assessment of what happened. Perhaps you were treated unfairly. Maybe someone did you wrong. It's natural to want to cling to the notion that you are right. It's validating. It feels good. For a while.

But "right" doesn't change what happened. It doesn't move you forward. It keeps you stuck in a place of resentment. Resentment feels awful. It's sullen and negative. Would you rather be "right" or would you rather be healed and move on to more pleasant experiences?

5. It Saves You from Taking Risks (or Any Actions) Today

"Oh sure, I *could* submit that proposal/painting/article to X...but it didn't work out last time I tried, so what's the point of trying again?"

This kind of thinking is a false justification for succumbing to fear or pessimism or laziness. It can squash your creativity, paralyze your actions, and stifle your progress. It can undermine your progress and growth. It can prevent you from pursuing new opportunities. It can block you from new, positive experiences.

6. It Protects You from Further Harm or Disappointments

The helpful part of your psyche uses thinking about the past as a warning flag. It wants to spare you from repeating past painful experiences.

Yet by interfering with your current activities, it is actually disrupting your present success and happiness...and curtailing the possibility of different outcomes occurring in the future.

7. Self-punishment

Some people have a deep-seated desire to punish themselves for negative events. It might not be conscious. It might be a long-term pattern of being hard on themselves. What about you? Be candid. Deep down, do you believe that if you make yourself feel bad enough about what happened for long enough, that you will be absolved somehow?

Punishing yourself for past experiences does not change what happened. Nothing will. Berating yourself serves no useful purpose.

However, you do have the opportunity to absolve yourself, through forgiveness. You can't change what happened but you can forgive yourself (and whoever else was involved) so that you can move on.

It's up to you. You can forgive yourself now...or you can do so after twenty years of "coulda woulda shoulda" self-flagellation. The only difference will be twenty years of feeling miserable... unnecessarily (more on this in Chapter 7).

KEY QUESTIONS

Using the same item you chose in the preceding set of questions (on pp. 13–14), answer the following:

- What benefits do you get from this regret or disappointment? Be candid.
- What attention and/or sympathy have you received from others?
- What does this past experience say about you? What qualities, skills, or talents does it reveal?
- Would you rather be "right" or would you rather be healed?

- To what extent do you give yourself permission to avoid taking actions now, based on what happened in the past?
- From what are you trying to protect yourself?
- To what extent do you punish yourself for what happened? What do you get out of your self-punishment? Why do you do it?

Are you ready to give up these apparent benefits? Are you motivated to end the toll of your regrets and disappointments? If so, begin by shifting your attention away from the past to focus on the present.

When you are ready, turn to Chapter 3.

CHAPTER 3

Shift Your Focus from the Past to the Present

If you have been carrying around the past—consciously or unconsciously—and would like to stop doing so, you need to shift your attention to the present.

To the extent you can think less about what happened in the past—and to the extent you can anchor your thoughts to what is happening now—the easier it will be to overcome your regrets and disappointments.

Let me repeat that: to overcome your regrets and disappointments, step one is to train yourself to think less about the past and to spend more time and energy in the present. Rather than focusing on specific incidents in your history, broaden your viewpoint. When you do, you can put past events in clearer perspective.

Thankfully, there are simple, proven techniques to shift your focus from the past to the present. For example, you can:

- Focus on the positive aspects of your current situation
- Train yourself to manage your thoughts, and,
- Cultivate mindfulness

FOCUS ON POSITIVE ASPECTS OF YOUR CURRENT SITUATION

Put aside the past for a moment. Bring your attention to your present life. No matter what you have experienced in the past, no matter what is going on in your life now, there is always *something* to appreciate. You are breathing. You have water to drink. You have food and shelter. You have a functioning brain.

Take a moment to take stock of the positive aspects of your current life.

KEY QUESTIONS

- What do you like best about your current life?
- What is going well for you these days?
- What are your favorite activities these days?
- Who are the people you enjoy being with?
- Where are your favorite places to spend time nowadays?

After you start identifying the good in your life, the next step is to appreciate it. Be thankful for it. Not only will it help anchor your focus in the present, it will also reduce stress, elevate your mood, and improve your relationships.

Even the middle of seemingly bleak times, opportunities for gratitude can be plentiful and profound. When Sean was dealing with kidney disease, he thought:

I'm so thankful for the actions of the medical personnel because they are doing everything they can to help me.

I'm so grateful for the researchers developing treatments because they are working on new ways to heal myself and others.

I'm so thankful this experience has deepened my relationship with my wife because our marriage is so much stronger.

Try it and see. Choose one of the items you mentioned in the preceding set of questions. Take a moment to feel gratitude for it. Doesn't that feel nice? Doesn't that feel better than regret or disappointment? The more you can feel positive and thankful, the more you will replace negative, unhelpful thoughts and emotions. The more you do, you will have a broader perspective that will help you overcome your regrets and disappointments.

Consider making gratitude a daily habit. It is a powerful practice to express thankfulness for what we have, who we are, and what we experience. There is a reason why gratitude is a central tenet in every spiritual practice on the planet: it works. It casts our lives in a more positive light. It shifts our focus to what's working well, rather than what is not.

Here are three simple, proven ways to make gratitude a regular part of your day:

1. Try a Daily Gratitude Practice

Begin a daily habit of listing your blessings, big and small. Ideally, begin your morning by writing out specific things for which you are grateful.

Why make gratitude a part of your morning routine? If you start focusing on thankfulness first thing, you will prime yourself to view your circumstances more positively throughout the day. You will center yourself by focusing on what you **do** like about your life, rather than racing around, stressing over what you **don't**. Which sounds more pleasant?

One caveat, though. Sometimes people try this practice and find that soon it deteriorates into a rote daily practice akin to writing out a shopping list. *(I'm grateful for my home, my meals, my friends, etc.)* If you've tried this practice and found it lacking, do what Einstein did: rather than just listing the things for which you are grateful, write out the reason **why**.

This small alteration—the additional explanation of *why* we're grateful—elevates and deepens each item exponentially. Rather than jotting down "*Terry's call*" on a laundry list of gratitude bullet points, it is much more powerful to specify the reasons. For example, *"I'm so grateful for Terry's call today because it felt so good to chat with a friend and I felt loved and cared about."*

Here are some other examples:

I'm so grateful for a good night's sleep because my brain and body are well-rested.

I'm so thankful the meeting went well yesterday because I believe our client is pleased and so is my boss. It was a good, gratifying experience for me and makes me feel more competent

I call this practice Gratitude 2.0. I could list dozens of jaw-dropping stories about the power of the practice of expressing daily gratitude...yet the best possible examples are from your own experience. Do yourself a favor: try it for yourself. See what happens.

TECHNIQUE
Gratitude 2.0

Each morning, write down at least five things for which you're grateful—and specify why.

I'm grateful for X because . . .

I'm so thankful for Y because . . .

Aim for at least five different items every day.

Optional Bonus Step:

After you make your gratitude list, re-read it. As you do, focus on really feeling thankful for each item. *(You might sense a little relief or some positive energy that heightens your gratitude. It is likely to feel good.)*

Once you start seeing the benefits of making gratitude a part of your morning routine, look for opportunities for thankfulness during the day.

2. Savor Special Moments throughout Your Day

Life is precious. No matter what is happening, little things can mean a lot. We can eat our meals mindfully, relishing each bite. We can sing along to a favorite song on the radio. We can take pleasure in the scent of our favorite soap. We can take comfort in a favorite chair. We can drink in a sunset or whatever else is visually pleasing to us. We can hold our loved ones a little closer in our minds and hearts.

By focusing on life's little pleasures, we foster more and more positive thoughts and feelings.

Chrissy Dunn found daily gifts as she conquered stage-three pancreatic cancer. "Every day is beautiful and I've learned to look at things as blessings that I used to just take for granted. The shoes I put on my feet, the hot water when I take a bath—every single aspect of my life is a blessing."

ACTIVITY

Today, make a point of savoring the simple pleasures you encounter. Eat mindfully. Enjoy the sensation of water on your hands when you wash them. Seek pleasant scents, sounds, and textures. Pause to take in the view, wherever you are.

Imagine that you have a 3D camera in your head. Whenever you see something, you want to capture, take a mental picture. Maybe you catch your kids or pets looking adorable Click! Perhaps you notice the lovely shape of the steam curling up from tea in your favorite mug Click! Oh, look at the way the sun is lighting up that building! Click!

TECHNIQUE

Internal 3D Camera

Pretend that you have a 3D camera in your brain. As you go through your day, take mental pictures of the scenes and moments you want to remember.

---

3. Appreciate the People and Things You May Have Been Undervaluing

As you have been focused on past events, consider what you may have been taking for granted in the present.

It wasn't until a car accident sidelined her that Judy realized how important her basic mobility was. Residents of Flint, Michigan, took clean drinking water for granted until they didn't have it when an unprecedented water crisis unfolded in 2014.

Also contemplate people you may have been taking for granted. Include people you know personally as well as strangers who provide you and others with goods and services.

Pay particular attention to the positive people in your life. Look for role models among the people around you. Who is looking on the bright side of things? Who has a great attitude?

Be aware and appreciative of the positive and helpful people in your life. Gravitate to them. Thank them. Spend the time you can interacting with them. Learn from them. Emulate them.

KEY QUESTIONS

- What have you been taking for granted? Make a list.
- Who have you been taking for granted? Consider people you know as well as strangers who provide you and others with goods and services.

- Who are the positive people in your life? What do you notice about them? What can you learn from them?

◆

MANAGE YOUR THOUGHTS

At any given moment, your busy brain is probably juggling a jumble of ideas, beliefs, and tasks.

What thoughts are occupying your mind right now? Are you making judgments? Are you criticizing yourself or others? Are you seeing the good in your current life? Are you doubting yourself? Are you comparing yourself to others? What kind of messages are you repeating to yourself? Are you spinning stories about "what might have been?"

You don't have to entertain every thought in your head, just as you don't have to eat every single item in a buffet meal. You can choose what you want to eat and ignore what you don't. You don't get upset or angry or frustrated that there are unappealing items in the buffet, you just leave them be. You can do the same with your thoughts.

You can learn to curate your thoughts. You can identify the ideas you want to harbor—those that are helpful and healthy. You can reject, ignore, or transform the ideas that don't feel good.

The thoughts and beliefs that are foremost in your mind play a major part in determining the nature of your current experience. However, most people are unaware of their inner dialog and how it is affecting them.

Pause for a moment to take stock. What's going on in your mind right now?

ACTIVITY

1. Set a timer for five minutes. Writing (or typing) as quickly as you can, jot down whatever thoughts enter your head.
2. When the timer buzzes, review your responses.
   - Put a check mark beside any thought that seems helpful or healthy.
   - Circle any thought that seems unhelpful or unhealthy.

Once you begin to pay attention to the thoughts occupying your mind, you can take steps to manage them.

If you think you can't control your thoughts, you are misleading yourself. For millennia, people have trained their brains using simple practices—and so can you.

Try any of the following techniques:

1. Foster Helpful, Healthy Thoughts

This is akin to the gratitude process in the previous section. Pay attention to what you **do** want to have in your head. Identify the kinds of thoughts and messages you would like to have guiding you.

Appreciate them. Savor them. Repeat them until they become prevalent in your mind. The more you do, the more you will generate more thoughts of this type. For example:

New opportunities arise every day. I make the most of them.

My life is getting better and better.

I am loved. I am lovable. The love I give returns to me tenfold.

Compile a "List of Good Thoughts" and keep them handy. You could jot them down on an index card or a page in your journal. You might keep them as a digital note in your phone or computer. What will work for you?

Going forward, capture new "good thoughts" as they occur to you. Add them to your list.

For the next few weeks (at least), read them every morning—and whenever you need a prompt to think more positively. Get yourself in the habit of reminding yourself of what you want to think and believe.

TECHNIQUE

List of Good Thoughts

---

1. Create a "List of Good Thoughts". Start with the items you've already identified in the previous activity. Add to them as new good thoughts occur to you.
2. Capture new "good thoughts" as they occur to you. Add them to your list.
3. Read your list every morning (and whenever you need a reminder of your preferred thoughts).

---

2. Notice Negative Thoughts and Comments

Implicit in your regrets and disappointments is criticism of yourself and others. You have developed a habit of judging things negatively—and that negativity takes its toll (as detailed in Chapter 2).

It is possible to interrupt this unhelpful habit. Step one is to begin to notice when you are being negative. Once you can recognize your judgment in the moment, you can take steps to address it.

Going forward, pay attention to the criticisms you make in your daily life —especially snap negative judgments about people, places, things, and activities. Some will be big and important—how you feel about your coworkers or yourself, for example. Many criticisms will be more innocuous: Maybe grammatical errors on public signs irritate you. Perhaps you are adept at finding flaws with restaurant meals or other people's attire.

TECHNIQUE

Notice Your Negativity

For the next thirty days, watch for any negative thoughts or comments.

Pretend it's like a game and you get points every time you notice you are making a critical thought. You earn bonus points when you notice in the moment. (It may sound hokey but, if you will suspend judgment and try it, rewarding yourself with points can be highly effective in facilitating personal changes.)

Warning: this may be challenging at first. You might be surprised by the scope and frequency of your negative thoughts, once you start paying attention to them.

"I didn't realize I was criticizing every little thing I experience," exclaimed Martina when she began the process. "I'm racking up lots and lots of points!"

3. Put Your Criticism in Perspective

Your criticisms are just your opinions. These thoughts are not gospel, science, the law, or the absolute Truth. It's merely the way you happen to view things at this point in time.

One easy technique to put your criticism in perspective is to add "in my opinion" to your statement.

For example, "Gosh, that's an ugly painting...in my opinion." Your criticism is only your opinion. It is not necessarily true. For all you know that painting might be at the cutting edge of an artistic wave that hasn't even been invented yet. Twenty years from now, you might look back at that painting and think, 'That's fantastic! How visionary! I love it!"

TECHNIQUE
"In My Opinion"

When you catch yourself criticizing someone or something—be it internally or aloud—immediately add the phrase "in my opinion".

Try this technique this week for yourself. See what you think.

When he tried it, Noel was struck at how this technique softened the harshness of his judgments. The shift from "Gosh that chatty clerk is annoying" to "Gosh that chatty clerk is annoying, in my opinion" offers up the possibility that someone else might find the chatty clerk to be more pleasant...possibly even delightful.

"Okay, this clerk isn't my cup of tea, but the elderly customer in front of me seems to be enjoying their conversation."

Next, look for other ways of viewing this thing you are criticizing.

1. Generate Alternative Interpretations

Consider that there are many other ways of viewing any situation. The more alternatives you can conjure, the better. The funnier, the more outlandish, the more effective they will be in putting your initial criticism in perspective.

For example, if your knee-jerk thought is something like, "Wow, what an awful outfit Taylor is wearing", consider some possible alternative interpretations:

(a) Taylor is dressing the best she can, given her pocketbook and taste.

(b) Taylor may be a fashion maven who is expressing herself in ways you're not appreciating.

(c) Taylor is so frazzled at work and home that she threw on whatever she had at hand and you're lucky she remembered to don her pants at all, and/or

(d) Taylor doesn't care a hoot about how her outfit looks so why should you?

This technique is especially helpful when you are critical of yourself. When my client Simone tried this technique, she found "Ugh! I messed up that presentation" was quickly translated into more palatable (and more realistic) alternatives:

Maybe I can't accurately assess the presentation's true value because I can't be objective.

Maybe the clients liked the presentation and were oblivious to the flaws I detected.

Maybe someone in the audience got something really important out of the talk so who am I to diss it?

This was a great opportunity for me to practice and to consider how I can give a better presentation next time.

TECHNIQUE
Generate Alternative Interpretations

Whenever you notice yourself criticizing someone or something, brainstorm a minimum of three other possible ways of reframing your original assessment.

Bonus points if you can make yourself laugh.

Once you begin the practice of generating alternative explanations, you can train yourself to do so automatically. When practiced over time, you can get to the point where, when you catch yourself making a criticism, you will quickly and easily counter with other options.

5. Suspend Judgment

The next level in addressing your negative thoughts and comments is to curtail your judgment altogether. You've done enough judging for one lifetime, so commit to doing less of it.

Constant criticism hurts you...and it's no picnic for people around you. The less you judge, the better for you and the people around you.

To the extent you can suspend judgment, you can allow events to unfold without the added, unnecessary energy of whatever label you've applied.

TECHNIQUE
Suspend Judgment

When you notice yourself making a judgment, stop.
Avoid labeling what you are experiencing.

It's not complicated. Simply cease judging everyone and everything. Rather than assessing, evaluating, and/or labeling, simply observe.

If you can't suspend judgment, delay it. (*Well, it seems weak to me at the moment but let's see what I think next month.*)

It's not complicated, but it can be challenging to suddenly cease judging altogether. Instead, look to curtail it. Aim to judge less often, less intently.

Aim for *progress*—for steady improvement over time—rather than expecting an unrealistic end state of "no judgments ever under any circumstances". You are human. You will make judgments. Aim to make fewer and fewer.

ACTIVITY

Practice Suspending Judgment

Choose a regular task you do in public (e.g. grocery shopping). This week, when you do it, make a point of watching the people there. Simply observe. When judgments pop into your head, push them gently but firmly aside.

Repeat this activity every time you engage in this regular task. Look for progress over time.

6. Accept What You Cannot Change

You might not like what happened. But it did happen. You can't change the past. Can you accept that fact and move on?

Acceptance doesn't mean that you approve. It means that you acknowledge the reality of what happened. *"Okay, that happened. I'm not happy about it but I can't deny what has occurred."*

Charlize Theron had to leave the Joffrey Ballet after a knee injury at twenty-one. She didn't have a choice. She had to accept that her dance career was over.

Look for ways to reduce or release the emotions you have about what happened. If you drop a glass and it breaks, you might be sad or angry for a minute. But then you must accept that the glass is broken. You clean up the shards and move on with your day. There isn't anything to be gained by continuing to feel angry or sad about the glass. Similarly, at some point, there is no value to spending emotions on your past regrets and disappointments.

This is especially vital with events or situations that you cannot change. (If you *can* change something, you can take actions to do so; more on that in Chapter 8.)

When you accept the things you cannot change, you rob them of their emotional charge. You put yourself in a better position to process them more objectively (Chapter 4), to let go (Chapter 9), and to move on with your life (Chapter 10).

TECHNIQUE
Acceptance

Consider your top regret or disappointment. Journal about it.

- To what extent can you change what happened?
- To what extent can you accept that this happened? It is over and done and is now a part of your history.

◆

CULTIVATE MINDFULNESS

Once you begin to curate your thoughts, you will be better positioned to cultivate mindfulness. This is perhaps the most important key to shifting from the past to the present—which is essential for overcoming your past regrets and disappointments.

Here's a quick activity to try, excerpted from Eckhart Tolle's book *The Power of Now*: stop and monitor your mind to see what your next thought will be. Close your eyes if you wish. Be very alert, ready to pounce on your next thought...as if you were a cat watching a mouse hole.

Please stop reading and do the activity. After you've given it a try, resume reading.

◆

How was that experience for you? If you are like most people, it takes a surprisingly long time for your next thought to materialize.

That gap? That time you spent, focused, waiting for your

next thought to emerge? That's an example of being present—of putting your attention in the here and now.

That period you spent waiting for your next thought is an example of mindfulness. It's a state of being totally focused on the present moment.

Right now, in this moment, all is well. The past and future are irrelevant. There is nothing to fear in the future because anything can happen between now and then. There is nothing to regret or dread from the past. The past is over and gone. Whatever regrets or disappointments that happened in the past are not actually happening to you right now.

The more you can focus on the present moment, the more you relieve yourself of your past burdens. If that sounds appealing, consider any of the following techniques to cultivate mindfulness.

1. Be

Take another break from reading to experience this. Sit for a moment and just "be". Clear your mind. Breathe. If you wish, close your eyes. For the next two or three minutes, focus on being here and now.

Please stop reading. Take a few moments to practice "being".

◆

How was that for you?

Most people experience a sense of relief when they try it. When you can put your attention on just "being," there is no pressure. There is no stress. There is no regret about the past. There is no anxiety about the future. You don't have to do anything. You don't have to think anything. You can just be.

Happily, this technique is infinitely portable and doable. Anytime you wish, you can simply stop and just "be".

This serves several important purposes: First, you'll feel better. Besides relief, you are apt to feel calmer and more like yourself.

Second, it separates you and your present circumstances from whatever happened in the past. Whatever regrets or disappointments may have occurred, they are not a part of this particular moment in time.

As soon as you establish this distinction between then and now, you are in a much stronger position to address and overcome your past regrets and disappointments.

2. Mini-meditation

The next step would be to make this a regular part of your day with meditation.

The psychological and physiological benefits of meditation are many and profound. Almost every bodily system functions better when you meditate regularly. Meditation has been proven to be an effective remedy for stress, low mood, depression, and anxiety. For many, meditation is also a spiritual practice that brings solace, comfort, and meaning to its practitioners. The added value of meditation is that it gives your brain a temporary break from the swirl of emotions and thoughts about your past burdens.

If you already have a meditation practice, wonderful! Please skip ahead to the next point.

If, however, you don't meditate, please read on. Despite all the potential benefits of meditation, what often stops people from giving it a whirl is the misconception that meditation requires grueling, boring and/or inconvenient l-o-n-g sessions. The truth is that you can derive all the psychological and physiological benefits of meditation through very brief sessions—just two or three minutes long—sprinkled throughout your day.

In fact, according to meditation guru Yongey Mingyur Rinpoche, it is better to aim for very short mini-meditation sessions than to tackle longer sessions.

How convenient! It's easy enough to take a two- or three-minute meditation break between tasks. It is not difficult. It is not complicated. It's just a matter of doing it. If you actually take a few brief meditation breaks every day, you will experience cognitive and health benefits.

The activity in the previous section is a mini-meditation. Let's add it to your tool kit of techniques. If you haven't yet tried it, please stop reading and give it a try now.

TECHNIQUE

Mini-Mediation

Set a timer for three minutes.

Sit quietly, eyes closed. Clear your mind. Breathe. Just "be". Gently push aside any thoughts that come up and refocus your attention on your breathing. Aim to think of absolutely nothing. When your mind wanders (and it will), avoid berating yourself. Simply clear your mind again. There is no wrong way to do this. Keep going until the timer buzzes.

Just as you can build bodily strength and skills by performing recurring fitness exercises, you can develop cognitive strength and skills by meditating regularly. If you did a mini-meditation, say, twice a day, every day, you could benefit every system in your body. The more you meditate, the greater the rewards. You are likely to feel happier and healthier and calmer. Try it this week and see.

3. Other Meditations

If you find the preceding techniques helpful, you may wish to expand your meditation practice. There are many, many ways to meditate. Try any of the following techniques for a week. See how it goes. Then try another for the next week. Over time, you'll find out what works best for you, under what circumstances.

Visual Meditation: select a beautiful image on which to concentrate. Sit upright in front of your chosen image and focus on it. Breathe. When your attention drifts, gently bring it back to the image.

Environmental Meditation: find a place outdoors that is attractive, peaceful, and safe. Breathe. Be present. One at a time, focus on each of your senses. What can you see? Hear? Smell? What can you detect with your skin?

Candle Meditation: light a candle. Set a timer for two or three minutes. Sit upright and focus on the candle flame. As thoughts occur to you, gently push them aside and refocus on the candle flame.

Walking Meditation: walk slowly and purposefully. As you do, put each foot down slowly and carefully. Direct your attention to your movement. When other ideas intervene, push them gently aside and refocus on your steps.

Body Scan: lie down on your back. Close your eyes and breathe. Direct your attention to your left foot. Slowly move your attention to your left ankle for a moment or two. Slowly shift your focus to your left shin, then later your left knee and eventually your left thigh. Repeat with your right leg. Continue the process, moving your attention slowly up through your torso, down each arm, up your neck and through your face and head.

Guided Meditations: there are ample options online, on CD or MP3 and via apps. The idea is to play the audio and follow the instructions as your thoughts are guided through specific imagery and instructions.

Try a Mantra: a mantra is a non-word utterance such as

"om" or "so-hum". These are ancient sounds that have a certain resonance, vibration, and history. As you meditate, close your eyes. Say or sing the mantra out loud. Feel the hum in your mouth and throat as you make the sound.

Try a Sutra: a sutra is a mantra that has meaning that is either uttered aloud or repeated silently, internally. It might be a single word such as "peace" or "love" or it might be a Sanskrit utterance such as "namaste" (the spirit in me recognizes the spirit in you) or "moksha" (I am emotionally free).

◆

If you'd like to learn more about meditation, here are some classic books on the subject:

Wherever You Go, There You Are: Mindfulness Meditation in Everyday Life by Jon Kabat-Zinn

Lovingkindness: The Revolutionary Art of Happiness by Sharon Salzberg

Joy of Living: Unlocking the Secret and Science of Happiness by Yongey Mingyur Rinpoche

Peace is in Every Step: The Path of Mindfulness in Everyday Life by Thich Nhat Hanh, with a foreword by Dalai Lama XIC and edited by Arnold Kotler

4. Monitor Your Presence

As discussed in Chapter 2, sometimes our past affects our present-day experiences in unexpected ways. Without knowing it, our past regrets and disappointments might be influencing our current relationships, careers, and general life contentment.

You might be carrying your past regrets into your current experience. Without meaning to, you might be emitting some residual stress or negative energy into your life now.

Check and see. Go to a mirror. Take this book with you. (Or hold your face in its current expression and snap a selfie. Resist the urge to mug for the camera—take a photo of yourself in this moment. You can delete it in a minute.)

What do you see? Are you projecting "Hey, what a great day! I'm loving life!" or "My life is a burden" or "Stay clear! You better not mess with me, pal" or something else?

How would you respond to the face you see in front of you?

How do you feel? What emotions are you aware of?

Are you carrying any tension in your face or body? Where?

Now, pretend it's your *best day ever*. Think of a particularly wonderful experience you've had—a glorious day that was a highlight of your life. Now—look at your face in the mirror again (or take another selfie).

What do you notice about how you feel and how you look now? How does it compare to how you felt and how you looked a moment ago?

If you've been carrying around the past—consciously or unconsciously—it probably shows in your face and demeanor. It might be affecting you now, more than you realize. It might be affecting how you feel and what you are communicating to others.

If you noticed a difference when you did the preceding exercise, you might benefit from monitoring your presence a few times a day. Pause and check yourself. Make any adjustments that make sense to shift your focus from whatever is on your mind to the present moment. Do you need to adjust your attitude? Is there some action that would be helpful for you to take? Do you need a break?

TECHNIQUE

Monitor Your Presence

Several times a day, check your expression. Either look into a mirror or take a quick, temporary, unposed selfie.

Examine how you feel in this moment and how you look.

Are any adjustments needed? If so, what?

---

5. Practice Shifting Focus to the Present

As you go about your day, look for opportunities to shift your attention to the present moment.

What are things that occur every day that you could identify as triggers to shift your focus to "now"? This might be regular activities you do, like brushing your teeth. You could take a moment to center yourself before you eat. You could aim to eat mindfully, savoring every bite.

You could use any phone calls or texts as a signal to pause and take a moment for yourself. Remember you are here, now, in the present.

If you drive, you might use stop lights or stop signs as visual cues to mentally, briefly, stop and be. Take a breath before you proceed.

TECHNIQUE

Shift Focus to Now

Choose an activity you do several times a day, every day. Begin a new habit: whenever you do this activity, pause and center yourself in the present moment.

---

6. Practice Relaxing and Releasing Stress

Take stock of any stress you are carrying right now. Do you need to release tension from your face, neck, shoulders, or elsewhere in your body?

If so, you might benefit from taking short breaks a couple of times a day to relax and release any physical tension.

Set some timers to go off randomly during the day. When they do, take a "Peace Pause". Breathe. Be in the moment. Survey your body and relax any area that is carrying any stress.

TECHNIQUE
Peace Pause

Set some timers to go off at random times during the day.

Whenever a timer buzzes, pause. Be present. Relax. Focus on your breathing for three normal breaths. Scan your body. Release any tension you detect.

Now that you have tools to anchor you in the present, you will be in a firmer position to examine what has happened in the past. When you are ready, turn to Chapter 4.

CHAPTER 4

Examine What Happened

Once you have taken stock of how your regrets and disappointments are affecting you (Chapter 2) and created some separation between your past and present circumstances (Chapter 3), you will be in a stronger position to address what happened.

Begin by conducting an objective review. As you go through the following steps, it is imperative that you actually write out your responses. Create a digital file you can type your responses into or grab a pen and paper or a journal. By writing your responses, you will elicit deeper insights and you will generate more ideas (including some surprises).

Pause after reading each step. Go ahead and write out your responses before reading the next step. Work through them at a pace that is comfortable to you. Take breaks when you need to.

1. Select One Regret or Disappointment That Is Affecting You Today

This might be an item from your list of burdens (p. 8) or it might be something else you've since become aware of. What still stings? What is hampering your current life?

2. Describe What Happened

In as much detail as you can, write down what happened.

- What led up to it?
- How did things unfold?
- What did you experience?
- How did you respond?

3. Challenge Your Account

Reread what you've written so far. Go through your description, one sentence at a time. As you do, ask yourself: is this really true? Is there another way of looking at this? How would an objective bystander view what happened?

For example: *"I blew my one chance to sell my screenplay and now I never will. How could I have made such a stupid mistake?!"* might be more realistically stated as *"I missed a great chance to sell my script but that wasn't the only possible opportunity to do so. There* will *be other opportunities in the future."*

For each sentence in your description, look for ways to dispute it. Generate other ways of looking at what happened.

Continuing with the same example: *"If I took some specific actions now, I could create new, possibly better opportunities to sell my script. A well written screenplay is always a hot commodity. It could be that I wasn't really ready before but now I'm more confident and therefore in a much stronger position to sell my script. Besides, I've since revised the screenplay a few more times so I know it's considerably better than what I had to offer earlier."*

If you get stuck, contemplate the following:

- What would your best friend say about what happened?
- If this had happened to someone you love, what would you tell them?

4. Consider That You Were Doing the Best You Could at the Time

When it happened, you relied on the skills you had at that time. You were limited by that knowledge and understanding you had then.

Consider the notion that you made the very best decision and took the very best course of action available to you at the time, under those circumstances.

Be candid. Remember what you were like when you experienced your regret. Think of the information you had available at that time. To what extent did you do your best, under the circumstances?

Sally and Rick had to sell their home in a difficult market. It took a long time to sell and they got less than they had expected. Two years later, property values jumped. "On the one hand, it kills me to think of the money we lost," says Sally. "But we had to sell when we did. We didn't have any other option. We couldn't have predicted that that the housing market would go crazy two years later. We did the best we could at the time. Actually, we were lucky to find a buyer at all, under the circumstances we were in."

5. Conduct a Reality Check

Most regrets and disappointments involve the implicit assumption that *if only* I would've done X (or not done Y), my life would now be much better, if not perfect. It is tempting to wonder (or fantasize) about alternative scenarios.

ACTIVITY

Make a list of the *IF ONLY*s you harbor concerning your regret.

- IF ONLY I would have . . .
- IF ONLY I hadn't . . .
- IF ONLY I would have said . . .
- IF ONLY I wouldn't have said . . .

The fact is, however, that your imaginary scenario is probably not true. If you would have done X (or not done Y), odds are slim that every single thing would have unfolded perfectly. You don't know what challenges or calamities may have befallen you along that untaken path. You don't know what good things you may have missed on the path you did take, had you gone the other way.

You are comparing your real life with its mixed bag of blessings to an ideal fantasy life that contains no problems at all. Is that fair?

Choose one of your *IF ONLY*s. Think of an alternative fate that seems more appealing...and imagine how this *IF ONLY* would have played out at that time.

For example: *if only I would have sold that screenplay, I'd be rich and successful now.*

Now be candid in extrapolating the "What if" scenario:

If I had sold that script, there is no guarantee that the movie would have been made. Very few are.

If it would have been made, there is no telling how the finished film would have turned out. It is likely that the studio executives would have made changes that I had no control over. They probably would have hired other writers to "fix" my script. It is likely that the resulting movie would have little in common with my original screenplay. It might end up being a terrible film, in which case my reputation as a writer would be damaged.

If I would have sold that script, there's no telling what would have happened in my personal life. Maybe people would be jealous or harassing me for favors to help get their screenplays sold. I don't know what challenges or pressures I would have faced. I can't guarantee I would have sold other scripts. I don't know what that life would have been like but I doubt that it would have been an easy, straightforward road to "rich and successful".

ACTIVITY

Choose one *IF ONLY* you harbor. Now imagine what *really* would have happened if you had done things differently. Play out the alternative fate as candidly as you can.

- Were you really in a position to do things differently?
- How would you have reacted, really?
- What might have been the likely consequences?

6. Realize That You Don't Have the Big Picture

Things just "are". From your limited point of view, you have no accurate way of assessing if a given event is truly "good," "bad," or anything else...and it is pretty much impossible to accurately determine which it is.

What seems like a terrific opportunity at first blush might end up, in the long term, being the worst experience of your life. Something that appears to be a massive setback might in fact be a way for you to deepen relationships and devise a better solution that yields a far more successful project.

For example, let's say a gallery offers to exhibit your work. That seems "good", right? Now imagine that there's a fire in the gallery and a lot of your work is lost. Now your exhibition seems "bad," right? But wait—because of the fire, let's say that you now get a lot of press and new commissions...well, then the original ill-fated exhibition seems "good". But what if you can't handle your newfound fame or you get swindled by unscrupulous financial managers or...you get the idea.

Sometimes "dreams coming true" are really nightmares. Sometimes "disappointments" are really "blessings in disguise". As things unfold, you have no accurate way of discerning what's actually happening.

All you know for sure is that this situation just "is."

Utilize the technique from p. 31: suspend judgment. Avoid labeling situations.

If you can't suspend judgment, delay it. *"Okay, right now I perceive it to be a bad thing. But maybe two or ten years from now, I'll see it differently. Who knows how things will unfold?"*

7. Apply a Statute of Limitations

Consider your top regret or disappointment. When did this event occur? Actually, write down the approximate date it happened as part of your description. (*Wait, how many years ago?*)

How much longer do you intend to brood over it?

Do yourself a favor by placing a limit on how long you let yourself dwell on what happened (or what didn't happen). *"Okay, I've felt badly about this for X years now. That's plenty. Time to move on."*

◆

Once you have examined what happened, it's time for the next step in *getting over it*—mining your experience for whatever good came out of it. That's the focus of Chapter 5.

CHAPTER 5

Seek Silver Linings

No matter how challenging the circumstances, good things happen.

Michael J. Fox was diagnosed with Parkinson's at age thirty, derailing a wildly successful acting career. He fostered good by founding a research foundation, becoming an advocate for people with Parkinson's, and writing inspirational books about staying positive, no matter what. He found new personal strength and an enriched, deepened relationship with his wife, Tracy Pollan.

Holocaust survivor Viktor Frankl noted the human kindnesses and simple pleasures he witnessed in the concentration camps. The beauty of a bird seemed so profound, he wept with joy to witness it. He turned down a chance to escape to stay behind and help people. In doing so, he found his own purpose in life and founded a school of psychotherapy (logotherapy) to help others do the same.

M. J. Ryan, (the author of wonderful books such as *Attitude of Gratitude*) explains how some gifts come wrapped in sandpaper: sometimes we receive something unpleasant, but when we get below the scratchy surface, there's something good there. A crisis might be an opportunity to draw closer to those involved. A loss allows us to appreciate what we had—and what we have.

I didn't get the role...but the experience will help me do better next time.

It was a dud of a workshop...in which I met my future business partner.

I lost my play when my hard drive crashed...but when I rewrote it, I created a much stronger third act.

To the extent that you can find the good things that came out of your past disappointment or regret, the easier it is to *get over it.* Try the following techniques:

1. Pan for Gold

Consider your top regret or disappointment. What good came out of this situation? Were there any "blessing in disguise"? Write down as many positive aspects or outcomes as you can.

Please pause and do the following activity right now.

ACTIVITY
Pan for Gold

Consider your top regret or disappointment. Complete the following sentences as many times as you can:

- I'm grateful it happened because...
- I'm thankful it happened because...
- This experience showed me...
- If I'm honest about it, it was a blessing because...

Now, how do you feel about what happened?

2. Appreciate the Positives of the Path You Have Taken

Rather than mourning "what might have been" or what didn't happen, focus on the good things you *have* experienced.

Consider what you might have missed out on, had you not experienced your top regret or disappointment.

For example, when she was twenty-four, Lisa turned down a "golden opportunity" to become a TV writer with a respected showrunner David Milch (*Hill Street Blues, NYPD Blues, Deadwood*). For years, she thought of that decision as her biggest regret...until she realized that, had she taken that path, she would have missed out on her corporate career in New York City, the experience of living in Paris for a decade, her current wonderful marriage, and a host of other elements that make her a better writer and a happier person today.

ACTIVITY

List five good things that are in your life now—or valuable experiences that you have had—that you would NOT have had if not for your earlier regret or disappointment. What blessings have arisen on the path you ***have*** taken?

3. What Did You Learn?

In every experience is the opportunity to learn. To grow. What did your regret or disappointment teach you?

KEY QUESTIONS

Consider what happened. What did you learn from the experience?

- What knowledge did you acquire?
- What insights did you gain?
- What did you learn about yourself?
- What did you learn about other people?
- What skills did you acquire?

- What did you learn to do differently?
- How did you grow personally and/or professionally?

If you are able to identify the lessons you learned relatively easily, wonderful! Please skip ahead to the next section.

If you are less clear about what you might have learned from the experience, take a moment to dig a bit deeper.

Here's the point: until you learn whatever lessons you can from what happened, you are at risk of repeating the situation. Think about someone you know who, say, keeps marrying and divorcing the same sort of person. Think about someone else who keeps creating the same drama over and over.

Life has a way of sending us the same circumstances over and over...until we learn from it. So, take this opportunity to stop the cycle by mining lessons from what happened.

Consider your regret or disappointment. Pretend you could go back in time, taking with you all the knowledge, experience, insights, and skills that you have today. What might you do differently in the same circumstances if you were the person, you are now?

TECHNIQUE

Coach Your Past Self

Consider what happened. If you could go back in time and coach yourself through whatever happened, what advice would you give yourself?

How might you apply the knowledge, experience, insights, and skills that you have today to that past situation?

Should a similar situation arise in the future, what might you do differently?

In what ways have you repeated your top regret or disappointment? Is there an opportunity here to change something going forward? What alternative solutions are there?

If you get stuck, consider how others might have handled what happened. What might they have done differently? Who is someone you respect and admire? What might they have done? What about your best friend—how might they coach you?

If you are not sure, ask. Present what happened to you as an anonymous hypothetical. Ask what they would do under those circumstances. They may give you new ideas, suggestions, or perspectives.

An essential part of *getting over it* is to mine the good out of whatever happened. Once you can see the silver linings in your regret or disappointment—once you can see the value of the lessons inherent in the situation—you're in a position to view what happened very differently. If you choose to, you can actually re-write the whole story. You can transform your words of woe into a tale of triumph. That's the opportunity in Chapter 6.

CHAPTER 6

Tell a Different Story

Words are the most powerful thing I know. They can change lives. They can soothe, nurture and teach—and they can also wound, irritate, enrage, and worse.

When we think of regrets or disappointments in our past, we tend to label them in the direst possible terms: *"I got fired!"; "I blew my ONE chance!"; "I'm an idiot!"*

Using these words means we are blaming and shaming ourselves rather than considering other aspects of the situation or circumstances that may have played a role in what happened.

When we catastrophize a past regret or disappointment, we tend to use words that make the event seem massive, permanent, and unchangeable. Research has proven that labels like these make us feel helpless and powerless to change the situation.

One effective step in *getting over* regrets and disappointments is to examine the labels we use to describe them—and to rewrite them as needed.

Think of it as being your own spin doctor.

1. Re-label Your Regrets and Disappointments

Take a past regret and ask if there's a more positive way to look at it. You didn't "get fired", you "left an uncomfortable job for an opportunity to be your own boss." You didn't "blow your one chance to sell your home," you "are actively seeking the right buyer".

Beginning with your top regret or disappointment, brainstorm alternative ways to refer to what happened. Be truthful. Be funny. Be hopeful. Play around with words until you find a way to refer to what happened with a label that is neutral, positive or—even better—empowering or inspiring.

ACTIVITY

1. How do you refer to your top regrets and disappointments? Write down the labels you use. How negative are these words? How harsh and overblown? What is the impact of these words on you?
2. Generate alternatives. How could you label what happened in a more neutral or positive way?

2. Re-label Yourself

While you are at it, consider the words you use to describe yourself. How do they affect you?

If somewhere deep inside, you call yourself an "idiot," how does that make you feel? How does that affect your attitude, decisions, actions, and self-worth?

It might be that you are carrying labels from long ago. These words can also shape how you think about yourself. For example, maybe when you were a kid, someone called you "scattered" or "bossy." Maybe it hurt. Perhaps you laughed. Either way, you may have inadvertently internalized the label.

ACTIVITY
Identify Your Self-labels

1. What labels do you use to describe yourself?
2. When you are angry or disappointed in yourself, what do you call yourself?
3. Write down some negative labels you recall from childhood.

Once you identify your self-labels, you can examine and process them. Question the validity of any hurtful or negative label. It might not be true. It might not be accurate. It might have been another person's opinion at that time—and probably said more about their issues and personality than it did about you.

The next step is to convert any negative label into a more helpful, more accurate one. For example, "scattered" could be rewritten as "interested in many things." "Bossy" could be re-written as "strong".

When I did this exercise, it triggered a clear memory of an occasion when an elementary school chum expressed her exasperation that I "start all these different projects and never finish any of them!" She called me a "flake". It hurt. This unexpected recollection revealed a negative label that, to my surprise, I'd been carrying deep inside for decades.

As soon as I identified it, I could question its validity. The truth is that, yes, I was involved in a lot of activities as a kid. Yes, I started many different projects. However, I finished many of them. (And what did my projects have to do with her? Why was she so bothered by them?) The cosmic truth is that no one *has* to finish *everything* they start. In fact, the physical reality is that it's absolutely impossible to do so.

Okay, my school chum thought I was a flake (and probably still does), but that label isn't accurate. I'm not a flake. I'm quite conscientious and responsible. However, I do have a lot going on. I do start a lot of projects. Some don't get finished and that's fine by me. A more accurate label would be that I'm "interested in many things." It's true! I am interested in many things! I'll shout it proudly!

3. Challenge Unhelpful Thoughts or Beliefs

Once you have addressed the negative labels you've been harboring, go deeper. Rewrite the unspoken script you have running inside your head.

Our brains are wired towards certain biases. When unwanted events happen, there can be a tendency to amplify them internally. We can think this situation is bigger and more damaging than it actually is or was. We can believe that it is permanent, rather than temporary. We can feel like we are doomed to repeat whatever happened or that because we failed once, we will never ever succeed.

The deal fell apart and I'll never find another buyer.

I blew my interview and I'll never get hired.

The producer turned down my script so I might as well stop trying to be a screenwriter.

Underneath these thoughts are deeper beliefs that can be affecting you more that you know. Consider how the following false beliefs might affect different areas of your life:

I must push, struggle, and toil to earn my success. If I'm not succeeding, I'm not trying hard enough.

Things never work out for me.

What unhelpful thoughts or beliefs are you holding? Scan your mind for negative notions. Pay particular attention to words like "always" and "never".

ACTIVITY

Consider your top regret or disappointment.

- What unhelpful thoughts do you have about it?
- What negative beliefs do you harbor, deep down?
- Dig deeper. What unhelpful beliefs have been interfering with your life?

Once you identify your unhelpful thoughts or beliefs, challenge them. They are not necessarily true. They are not law, science, or gospel. They are just notions in your head.

Consider the alternatives. The previous examples could be rewritten more accurately as follows:

This deal fell apart so I need to find another buyer. There are plenty out there. I might even make a better deal.

My interview didn't go well but I learned a lot from the experience that I can use during future job searches. It was only one interview. There are many other opportunities available. I know that I will get hired.

The producer turned down my script I need to get this and other scripts in front of other producers.

Sometimes things don't work out for me. Often, they do.

I can't "buy" success by suffering. Many people experience success with less effort and less strife. Success does not necessarily require struggle and toil.

TECHNIQUE

Challenge Unhelpful Thoughts and Beliefs

1. Select one item from your list in the preceding activity. Write out as many refutations as you can.

    - Is this really true?

- What evidence is there to the contrary?
- What is the objective reality? What is the real truth here?
- What would you rather believe?

2. Rewrite this item. What would be a more helpful way to phrase it?

---

4. Rewrite Your Story

Similarly, there is more than one way to view negative incidents in your past.

Here is one story: *I was fired from a job I loved. I was blindsided. It wasn't fair. I was going full tilt, eighty hours a week, doing good work. Maybe too good. I suspect some of my colleagues conspired to oust me. I was stupid to have trusted them. I tried to apply for other jobs but nothing panned out. I had to go into business for myself. It's okay but not as lucrative. I feel like I blew my career. I get angry when I think about what I could have done with the extra money. I feel like such a loser. I got fired ten years ago and it still feels like a dagger in my back.*

Here's a different version of the same story: *Losing my job was the best thing that could have happened to me. I got out of an organization where I didn't fit. I escaped from a stressful environment and from people who didn't appreciate me. I got to start my own business, which is a huge accomplishment. I'm independent. I can do whatever work I want. My schedule is my own. I make less money but I also work half the hours, meaning I have time for my family and for personal pursuits. For the past ten years, I've been healthier, happier, and much less stressed than I was when I worked for that company. My life is much better now than it would have been, had I stayed in that job.*

Again, words matter. You could label the first version as the story of a "corporate victim", whereas the second version is the story of an "entrepreneur who turned a setback into a triumph".

If this was your story, which version would you prefer?

When looking back at a disappointment, you have a choice about how you tell what happened. You can tell a tale of woe... or you can spin it more positively. You can bore people by chronicling how, exactly, you were victimized and by whom...or you can find the funny in it. Or the lesson. Or the motivation to take action. Or a new opportunity.

"The producer said 'no'" can become a side-splitting comedy monologue...or the seeds of a production company of your own... or inspiration to create a practical workshop for others.

What story would you like to be telling about what happened? "I failed" or "I learned" or "I found a creative solution" or something else?

When Matt Damon and Ben Affleck were fledgling actors, they were repeatedly rejected for the roles they wanted. They could have given up. They could have become bitter. They could have resigned themselves to only acting in minor roles. They could have quit acting and sought careers outside of show business. Instead, they wrote a screenplay, *Good Will Hunting*, which not only won them an Academy Award, it gave them access to the kinds of film roles that had been eluding them.

When you rewrite your story, you take control over it. You can decide to shed the negative elements you've been bearing. You get to choose how you want it to affect your current life.

Consider how much better you might feel about what happened if you told a different story about it.

For example: *"I regret that I never finished college"* might be more helpfully stated as *"School was a lower priority than other things at the time. I did what was right for me at the time. My path was different but I've learned a lot along the way. If I wanted to, I could take classes now. If it's truly important to me, I could work toward a degree. I've seen news articles about people in their eighties and nineties who do just that. Actually, I might appreciate it more now. I would be a better student now than I would have been then."*

TECHNIQUE
Rewrite Your Story

---

1. Select a past regret or disappointment that still hurts. Clear some time to literally rewrite that story. What's a non-victim version of what happened?
    - What is the best possible version of what happened?
    - What good came out of the experience (Chapter 5)? How can you incorporate that into your story?
    - How can you reframe negative aspects into neutral or positive terms?
    - Can you view what happened through a comic lens?
    - What if you were to use what happened as the basis for an inspirational movie—what would that story be like?
2. Reread what you have just written.
    - What is the tone of this story? How positive and uplifting? What adjustments are needed?
    - Are there any negative words or phrases? Any hints of blame or victimhood? If so, edit them.
    - Play with the phrasing until you have a version that feels really good.
3. Reread your rewritten story every day for the next week.
4. Going forward, if you find yourself sliding back into thinking

about your old version of the story, pause and pivot. Remind yourself of your rewritten, preferred version.

Once you reframe your regret or disappointment into a more helpful story, it makes it relatively easy to forgive yourself and others involved. That's the next essential step to *get over it.*

When you are ready, turn to Chapter 7.

CHAPTER 7

Forgive Yourself and Others

An essential, unavoidable part of *getting over* regrets or disappointments is to forgive yourself and others for whatever happened. Forgiveness and self-forgiveness aren't always easy, but the benefits are many and profound.

◆

WHAT CAN FORGIVENESS DO?

Whenever you sincerely forgive yourself and/or others, you have the opportunity to:

- Release grudges and resentments
- Overcome regrets, disappointments, and past mistakes
- Dissolve guilt, blame, and shame
- Disrupt unhealthy or unhelpful thought patterns
- Disrupt unhealthy or unhelpful behavior patterns
- Accept things you cannot change
- Resolve conflicts
- Improve relationships
- Feel better about yourself

FORGIVE OTHERS

"Not forgiving others" is one of the three most common regrets hospice chaplain Tenzin Kiyosaki reports that she hears from patients who have less than six months to live. "If you just clear the regrets," she says, "you have so much more open heart and receptivity to the world."

Think about your own experience of forgiving someone. There is a visceral release of bad feelings you've harbored against this person. There is a sense of relief. There is a new, more positive feeling towards them. There is a palpable improvement in the relationship.

Remember a time you were forgiven. Recall your gratitude at being able to get past something you regretted doing. Think about the release of the burden you were bearing.

Mechanically, forgiveness is easy. You simply do it.

In practice, it can be more challenging because our clever minds want to protect us from further harm. When someone hurts us, our protective brains want to hold the other person accountable. But forgiveness is not approval for what occurred. Forgiveness is not "letting someone off the hook." Forgiveness is an acknowledgement that we all make mistakes.

"But you don't understand," you may protest. "They were wrong! They hurt me badly! Why should I forgive them?" Well, ask yourself this: would you rather be right or would you rather be healed? If you want to heal, you must forgive them.

Let's say you've been wronged. Someone was involved in your past regrets and disappointments. What are your options?

1. You can stew—keep it all inside, festering. That only hurts yourself. It takes its toll, mentally and physically.

It colors your interactions with other people. It makes it difficult for you to trust others.

2. You can play the victim. You tell everyone about the horrible thing that happened to you—spread the word about the terrible person who hurt you. This only foments negativity and spreads the pain. Worse, it keeps you stuck in an unhelpful, unproductive place. It prevents you from moving forward and from creating new, better experiences.
3. You can lash back—seek revenge or payback. This may give you momentary satisfaction but it won't feel nearly as satisfying as you anticipate—and it will not heal your pain.
4. You can forgive them and move on. If you want to heal—if you want to *get over it*—forgiveness is the answer.

Consider the story of Bill Pelke, a retired Alaskan steelworker. Four teenage girls murdered his grandmother in 1985. Initially, when the fifteen-year-old ringleader, Paula Cooper, was sentenced to die in the electric chair, Bill approved. Subsequently, he underwent a spiritual transformation. He prayed for love and compassion for Paula and her family. He not only forgave her, he led an international crusade on her behalf to remove her from death row. As a result, Paula's sentence was commuted from death by electric chair to sixty years in prison.

Bill went on to co-found a non-profit organization called Journey of Hope, an international group of "death row family members, family members of the executed, death row survivors, activists, and friends" who work to promote non-violence and forgiveness. As an alternative to the death penalty, they promote "restorative justice"—a process that fosters "offender accountability and the opportunity for the offender to make things right with the victim as much as possible."

If Bill Pelke can forgive the woman who killed his beloved grandmother, is it possible for you to forgive the people involved in your past regrets and disappointments?

ACTIVITY

Make a list:

- Who do you need to forgive?
- Who do you hold responsible for your regrets and disappointments?
- What grudges and resentments are you holding?
- With whom are your angry?
- For what?

Truthfully, forgiveness lets YOU off the hook. It's a way to release the pain, the anger, the fear, and the resentment you experience when someone hurts you. Forgiveness gives you the opportunity to heal and move on.

Besides, the alternatives do not work. Lashing back or seeking revenge is never as satisfying as you imagine. Harsh actions injure you in the long run. Holding grudges and hard feelings against those who have harmed you hurts you much more than it affects them.

The longer you let resentments fester, the more you are damaging your own happiness. It is impossible to be happy if you are bearing burdens from the past. Who does it serve if you are walking around, bitter and seething about something that happened a decade ago...while the person who hurt you can't even remember your name, let alone the incident? Grudges hurt you, not them.

"But it's too late," you may say. No, it isn't. It's better to forgive late than not at all. You can be way overdue when it comes to forgiving others. And as soon as you do, you can heal. Plus, you can't truly move forward until you forgive.

"But I don't even know where they are, what they're doing, if they are even alive," you might counter. It doesn't matter. If you can forgive someone in person, it's powerful. But you can also forgive someone without them knowing anything about it. It doesn't matter where they are or what they're doing—you have the power to forgive them, right here, right now.

Forgiveness is really a gift you give yourself. You'll feel the difference in your own heart when you truly forgive someone. There's a little shift, deep down. There is a sensation of release as the burden begins to lift. It feels like relief. It's the first step to replacing the pain of the incident with peace and joy.

Forgiveness is a very simple, very powerful process but sometimes it can be challenging. See if the following activity is helpful.

FORGIVENESS ACTIVITY

Clear some uninterrupted time for personal reflection. Select one person you need to forgive from your list from the previous activity (p. 65). With this person in mind, answer the following questions:

1. What grudges or resentments are you holding against this person?
2. What is it costing you to hold these resentments? How does it make you feel?
3. How do these grudges and resentments affect how you are living your life?
4. How do these grudges and resentments affect the people around you?
5. How do these grudges and resentments affect the person you are holding responsible?

6. What benefits might there be to forgiving this person? How would you feel? How might it improve your life?
7. Imagine this person as a child, helpless and alone. To what extent could you have compassion for them in that circumstance?
8. Recognize that this person is a fallible human being, susceptible to making mistakes like everyone else on the planet, including you. Consider that we all do the best we can at any particular moment, given the skills, knowledge, and understanding we have at that time. We would all like to be forgiven for the mistakes we've made.
9. Consider what this person did. In what ways might you have done something similar? *(E.g., if they lied to you, ask in what ways have you been dishonest in your life?)*
10. Remind yourself that forgiveness is not approval or justification for what happened.
11. Forgive this person. Take a moment. Acknowledge that they are a fallible human being. View them with compassion and kindness. Decide to forgive them. Act accordingly.

FORGIVE YOURSELF

Now, it's one thing to forgive someone else. But it's quite another to forgive yourself.

Many of us are hard on ourselves. We punish ourselves for mistakes we've made. We berate ourselves for things we did or didn't do.

But if we insist on carrying negative experiences from our past, we are needlessly denying ourselves happiness in the present. Without meaning to, we are limiting ourselves by curtailing our progress forward.

ACTIVITY

For what do you need to forgive yourself? Make a list.

We need to forgive ourselves. We deserve to be treated kindly and compassionately—especially by ourselves. As human beings, we all make mistakes.

Whatever it is, forgive yourself. You deserve the same courtesy you would give someone else.

Imagine the relief of truly forgiving yourself! Picture yourself laying those unnecessary burdens down...and moving forward with your life. Rather than berating yourself for things you can't change, wouldn't you prefer to be spending that energy on something more pleasant, healthy, or helpful? Wouldn't you rather move forward into fresh, new experiences?

What is stopping you? What has been preventing you from releasing this burden? Why are you punishing yourself?

Is it guilt? Do you need to apologize or ask for someone else's forgiveness before you can truly forgive yourself? Then do so.

If there is no way to reach or request forgiveness from someone, do the next best thing: write out an apology. Be sincere.

Are there any amends you can make? If not to the actual person, is there something you could offer to your community, instead?

What follows is a self-forgiveness activity you can use to work through each item on your list. For best results, choose only one item and answer the questions. Forgive yourself. Wait at least a day until you address another item on your list.

Note that you may have answered the first two questions in previous activities in this book. Go ahead and answer them again.

(You may find you have new insights to add now.) Then take a step farther to forgive yourself.

SELF-FORGIVENESS ACTIVITY

Clear some uninterrupted time for private reflection. Select one item on your list. Answer the following questions:

1. What does it cost you to carry this burden? How does it affect different areas of your life? Your relationships? Your attitude? Your health? Your level of stress?
2. What does it cost others around you?
3. What benefits would there be to forgiving yourself? How would you feel? How would it change how you are living your life?
4. What has been stopping you from forgiving yourself? Why are you denying yourself this relief?
5. What needs to happen for you to forgive yourself?
6. Are there any apologies or amends to be made? If so, make them.
7. Take a moment. Acknowledge that you are a fallible human, that you make mistakes (as we all do), and that you deserve forgiveness for them. Consider that you do the best you can at any particular moment, given your skills and understanding at that time. View yourself with compassion and kindness. See yourself as a small child. Forgive yourself.

CHAPTER 8

Take Action

At this point, you've already had the opportunity to take some specific actions to get over your regrets and disappointments. You can:

- Take stock of how your past regrets, disappointments, and mistakes are affecting you today (Chapter 2)
- Shift your focus from the past to the present (Chapter 3)
- Examine what happened (Chapter 4)
- Look for the good in what happened (Chapter 5)
- Tell a different story (Chapter 6)
- Forgive yourself and others (Chapter 7)

Now consider what other actions you can take to *get over it*. Chart a course that will give you relief. This might mean devising a new plan to accomplish something that didn't work out for you... or abandoning an earlier goal and trying something completely different.

Any action will feel much better than dwelling on something in the past you can't change.

1. Identify Your Options

Whenever disappointments arise, you have options:

If something didn't yield the result you wanted, **you can try again**. It took Thomas Edison over 1,000 tries to perfect the light bulb. Colonel Harland Sanders's infamous chicken recipe was rejected 1,009 times before he found a restaurant to accept it. Although Emily Dickinson published only had a handful of poems during her lifetime, she kept writing…leaving almost 1,800 completed works. Winston Churchill lost every election for public office in which he ran...until age sixty-two when we became prime minister of England. Jack London's first story was rejected 600 times before the author of *Call of the Wild* and *White Fang* finally found a willing publisher.

You can try doing the same thing a different way: R.H. Macy's first seven businesses failed before he created a successful enterprise in the form of Macy's department store.

You can find a new path to your destination: as mentioned in Chapter 6, Matt Damon and Ben Affleck weren't having much success with the traditional route to getting acting work (i.e., auditions), so they tried something different: they wrote a screenplay (*Good Will Hunting*) and in so doing, they completely changed the trajectory of their careers.

You can try something completely new: when he retired from the army, Bob Ross started painting...and ended up becoming an icon on American public television and beyond.

Another option is to give up: you can purposefully decide that you no longer wish to follow this particular path. When he was a teenager, Joe had his heart set on being a famous musician. But his initial attempts revealed that he hated the marketing and the touring and the practical implications of that life. He chose to give up that dream and to pursue a musical career through teaching, which was much more pleasant for him.

What alternatives are there for proceeding in your particular case? What makes sense under the circumstances? Try not to let your ego decide. What does your gut say?

Before you decide, dive a little deeper. Consider less obvious options.

What are you avoiding? As described in Chapter 2, when we experience regrets or disappointments, there is a natural, understandable tendency to protect ourselves from repeating those painful or negative occurrences.

In an effort to protect ourselves, we may give up prematurely. We may steer clear of certain people, places, situations, or activities. When Lynn was fired unexpectedly, she retreated altogether from the corporate world. She made a couple of half-hearted applications for new jobs but had lost all her confidence. Having been fired, she didn't think another company would want her. And she was scared. She didn't want to risk being fired again.

What else might you be missing? In hunkering down and focusing on past regrets or disappointments, have you been missing other, new opportunities? Maybe you have been so focused on your initial goal, you haven't seen other, more appealing options.

Do some research. Educate yourself about your current opportunities. If you were to start fresh now, what might you do?

This is more difficult to discern so get help. Ask people you trust what they see as your current options. What new opportunities do they see unfolding in the world?

TECHNIQUE

Identify Your Current Options

1. Make a list of your current courses of action. Include:
   - Trying again.
   - Doing the same thing a different way.
   - Trying something completely new.
   - Giving up.
2. Add to your list. What have you been avoiding?
3. What else might you be missing? What new opportunities might appeal? *If you are not sure, do some research. Ask people you trust for their ideas.*

2. Prioritize and Choose

Once you have identified and surveyed your current options, make a choice about how you would like to proceed.

You need to move forward. What action would you like to take at this time? What is most appealing to you? What is most interesting?

ACTIVITY

Make a decision about how you would like to proceed at this point in time? Which of your options is most appealing? Choose your preferred course of action.

3. Take Action

As soon as you decide your path forward, take action.

If in doubt, choose the easiest possible steps forward. Write a page. Make a phone call. Do the thing you've been avoiding for, say, ten minutes.

ANY action will feel so much better.

ACTIVITY

1. Consider your preferred course of action.
   - What needs to happen?
   - What actions can you take?
   - What are the simplest, easiest steps forward?
2. Stop reading and take action. Right now. Set a timer for ten minutes. Spend this time taking action.

4. Eliminate Reminders of Your Past Regrets or Disappointments

Once you start moving in your preferred direction, do a little clean-up from the past.

What are you holding onto that reminds you of your past regrets or disappointments? Go through your living space. Remove anything that feels negative or otherwise icky. Shred those rejection letters. Donate that jacket you wore on that bad day. Delete the contact information for that person who let you down.

Imagine that you are pressing a reset button. You get to start fresh right now. Leave behind anything that doesn't feel good. Jettison whatever doesn't suit the "new you".

How is your attire? Are you dressing in clothes that fit and flatter and feel good? If so, great! If not, use this as an opportunity to treat yourself better. Prune your wardrobe of items that don't do you any favors, mentally, emotionally, or physically. Donate items to people who will make better use of them.

Next consider the information you are keeping. You may need to retain certain paperwork or digital files for tax, legal, or other reasons. Put them someplace where they are safe but removed from your daily attention. Triage the rest. Eliminate what is not helpful, pleasant, or necessary. Shredding unneeded paperwork can feel great.

Delete items from your phone that you don't or won't need. If in doubt, put a copy of the information somewhere you can retrieve it if necessary—but spare yourself the impact of carrying around contacts, texts, or photos that have negative connotations for you. Why carry around reminders of past regrets or disappointments literally in your pocket?

It might be that you can't bear to part with a "failed" project, given the time and energy you poured into it. That's understandable. Instead of destroying it, find a way to retain it while framing it more positively. For example, you could collect all the relevant materials into a binder or box and label it "Learning Project #4". Be proud of what you put into the project and what you learned along the way.

Author Barbara Sher used half-inch binders for this purpose. Whenever a project didn't pan out, she put the materials in a binder as a way of honoring the work and thought she had put into it. By saving the material in this way, it didn't feel like she had wasted her time or effort. Over time, she amassed a shelf full of former projects that was almost as gratifying as the shelf of the books she published.

Get rid of anything that you don't want to carry into your future. Eliminate negative reminders and leave them behind. Or transmute them into more pleasant, more positive mementos—lessons learned, say, or "A great idea that was super fun to work on while it lasted."

ACTIVITY

Eliminate Negative Reminders

Take a moment to visualize the person you are now choosing to be.

Now, go through your living space. Remove anything that doesn't feel good. Jettison or donate anything that doesn't suit your preferred self.

- Are there any objects that remind you of your regrets or disappointments? Donate them, sell them, or discard them.
- Do you have any clothing that doesn't fit or flatter you or carries negative connotations? Donate them.
- What about paperwork and digital files?
  - Retain what you need for legal, tax, or other purposes.
  - Store it so that it is safe but removed from your daily attention. What can you get rid of? Shred it or delete it.
  - Is there a "failed" project you invested a lot of time and effort in? If you don't want to get rid of it, transform it into something more positive. Bundle it up and re-label it (e.g., *Learning Project #4*" or "*A great idea I had a blast working on*").
- Edit your phone. Remove any contacts, texts, or images that remind you of regrets or disappointments. If in doubt, store a copy somewhere you can access it if needed—but cease carrying it around in your pocket.

When you eliminate negative reminders, you make it easy to let it go, which is the focus of the next chapter. You are clearing a space for you to receive better, more helpful, more pleasant experiences. You are shedding your past regrets and disappointments to foster a better future.

CHAPTER 9

Let It Go

If you haven't already done so, it's time to let go of your past regret or disappointment. Whatever happened, it is time to move on. Avoid staying stuck by letting go.

1. Make a Conscious Decision to Let Go

Take a moment to contemplate your top regret or disappointment. Actively choose to cease expending any further time, effort, or thought on what happened.

Say out loud, "It's time to let go of ____________."

Relax. Release your burden. You might say or think something like:

I am willing to let go.

I release all thoughts and judgments about what has happened.

I release all tension. I release all frustration, all anger, all guilt.

I let go and I am at peace. I am at peace with myself. I am at peace with my current situation. I am at peace with Life.

I am safe.

If it helps, write down your regret or disappointment on a piece of paper—then destroy it. Rip it up, shred it, or burn it. As you witness the physical destruction of the paper, remind yourself. "It's over. It's gone. It's done. I'm finished with it. I'm moving on."

2. Act As If It Never Happened

Pretend that this burden in your past never existed. Try this now: imagine if that regrettable incident never happened. For a moment, close your eyes and pretend it never happened. Breathe.

How do you feel?

Now, declare today your "Fresh Slate Day". For the entire day, act *as if* you are free of your burden from the past.

If that feels good, continue with this practice tomorrow and the day after that and hey, why not for the rest of the week? Grow accustomed to living without this burden from your past. Be free of it.

3. Monitor Your Mood

How you feel is an efficient signal for what is going on internally. Should you find yourself feeling "off" or down or stressed or troubled or otherwise "icky", pause. Ask yourself: what is going on? What emotions am I feeling?

Scan your body. Release any tension you detect. Take some deep breaths.

Now ask: does what I'm experiencing feel like something in my past? Am I dwelling on past regrets, disappointments, or events?

If so, process your thinking (Chapter 4 may help).

4. Curate Your Thoughts

If you catch yourself thinking about past regrets or disappointments, stop yourself by gently shifting your attention to something more positive.

Avoid berating yourself. Just realize "Oops, I'm thinking about something that isn't helpful" and shift your attention elsewhere.

Consider your options. At this moment in time, you can dwell in the past or you can focus on something in the present. Make a conscious choice. Pivot in a new direction that feels better.

Use the techniques in Chapter 3 to shift your focus to the present. Replace negative thought or unhelpful beliefs with more positive, helpful notions. What would you rather have in your head?

Concentrate on the task at hand. Be present.

If your mind continues to drift to your past regrets, remind yourself of any silver linings (Chapter 5). Read your revised story of what happened (Chapter 6).

5. Disrupt Negative Thinking Loops

Do you latch onto a negative thought and mull it over and over and over again? Or fixate on how to retaliate for an unpleasant occurrence—for example, mentally composing and recomposing harsh restaurant reviews to get revenge for a bad meal? Or do you replay an upsetting conversation over and over? (*Ugh! I should have said X or Y or Z at the meeting! I could have said X or Y or Z! Why didn't I say X or Y or Z?*)

Thankfully, these are only thoughts. Just as you have the power to create them, you have the power to stop them and/or to change them.

Stubborn negative thinking loops may require you to confront them in overt ways—for example by saying "Enough!" out loud.

Process what you are thinking. Is this thought accurate? If not, rephrase it so it is. Now dispute it. What evidence is there to the contrary? What would a neutral party say about it?

How else could you look at this? Generate (at least) three alternative thoughts.

Reach for any thoughts that feel better.

Distract yourself with another activity to occupy your mind. What activities do you find engrossing? For example, you could read an engaging book or tackle a jigsaw puzzle or call a friend to talk about anything else other than the repeating thought in your head.

If you find yourself dwelling on your "favorite mistake" too frequently or repetitively, try wearing an elastic band around your wrist to snap whenever thoughts about the regret recur. (It may sound silly but it really does work.)

TECHNIQUE

Disrupt Negative Thinking Loops

---

1. Interrupt your thought pattern.
   - Say "enough!" out loud. Hold your hand up like a stop sign. (This may even make you giggle, which can break the loop.)
   - Change your body posture (for example, stand up if you are seated). If possible, change your physical location.
   - Take a few conscious breaths.
2. Process and transform your thoughts.
   - Rephrase for accuracy.
   - Dispute it.
   - Generate at least three alternatives.
3. Choose a thought—any thought—that feels better. Write it out ten times. Say it out loud. Put a tune to it and sing it. Get your brain hooked on the new thought.
4. Distract yourself. Engage in an engrossing activity to give your mind something else to do.
5. For the next day or so, wear a thick elastic band on your wrist. Whenever your negative thought recurs, snap the elastic. It

will hurt (briefly) and will immediately interrupt the loop. It may seem odd but if you do this for a few days, you will train your brain to avoid this thought.

Have You Let Go?

If so, great! You can either skip ahead to the next chapter, or select a different regret or disappointment to process, beginning with Chapter 4.

If not—if you haven't yet released your burden, why not? What is stopping you?

KEY QUESTIONS

If you are still having difficulty letting go, journal answers to the following questions:

- Were you doing your best at the time? Did you take the decisions and actions that you could, given your knowledge, skills, and understanding that you had at the time?
- Are you punishing yourself? Why?
- Have you formed a habit so deeply ingrained, you can't break it? Are you addicted to a pattern of regret you have created?
- Are you being influenced by others? Is someone reinforcing your need to hold onto this regret or disappointment?
- What benefits are you getting from holding onto your burden and what is it costing you? (Consider the items in Chapter 2.)
- What would it take for you to let go? Under what circumstances would you release this burden?
- Would you rather be "right" or would you rather be "healed"? If the latter, you have to let it go.

Note: if the techniques in this section are insufficient to help you let go, you may need professional help to do so. Consider working with a counselor, psychologist, or life coach. You're worth it.

CHAPTER 10

Move Forward

Once you let go of your past regrets or disappointments, you have an opportunity to purposefully choose how you want to be living your life, going forward.

Okay, this unwanted event occurred in the past. You've dealt with it and let it go. Now, pause to consider: how do you want to operate going forward?

If you choose to, you can use this as a pivot point to:

- Treat yourself well.
- Recognize and utilize your strengths.
- Accentuate the positive.
- Choose your path forward.
- Manage your expectations, and
- Deal more effectively with any future regrets or disappointments.

◆

TREAT YOURSELF WELL

Do you take good care of yourself? Do you eat nourishing food and take proper care of your health? Do you give yourself treats, including time for your favorite personal pursuits?

What does your attire say about you? Are you well-groomed and wearing clothes that fit and flatter you? We touched on this in Chapter 8 but let's go deeper: are you presenting yourself as someone who values themselves or are you signaling a lack of self-respect?

If you take great care of yourself, excellent! Please skip ahead to the next section.

If, however, you tend to be hard on yourself, pause and consider that you are worth treating better. When you fully appreciate yourself and treat yourself well, you will feel so much better! You will be in a much stronger position to overcome challenges, achieve your goals, and get more out of life.

Start with the basics. How can you treat yourself better?

ACTIVITY

1. Brainstorm answers to the following questions:
   - Given your current life, what could you do to take better care of your health and body?
   - What treats could you give yourself?
   - If you gave yourself time for yourself, how would you spend it?
2. Circle the items that are most appealing.
3. Find ways to treat yourself well, going forward.

Next, consider how you tend to talk to yourself. What kind of messages tend to replay in your mind? What is your tone like? Are you harsh or supportive of your efforts? Are you your own head cheerleader or do you tend to criticize yourself?

There is nothing wrong with holding yourself to a high standard...however, your inner critic can do real damage if it is left to run rampant. It says things like, *this is doomed to fail* or *I'm an idiot* or *things never work out the way I want.*

Your inner critic operates at a deep, subconscious level. It does not respect you and seeks to sabotage you. You must teach it to value you by putting it in its place when it surfaces.

It may sound like someone from your past—or it might not. I call my own inner voice Picky McStrict. My coaching clients use names like "Sir Harps-a-lot", "Ursula", "Poopyhead", "Nick the Dick", "Lady Gwendolyn", "El Stupido", and "Mr. Dibbs My Grade Two Teacher".

Examine your inner critic. What does it say? How does it say it? Does it sound like anyone you know? What is it afraid of?

Once you get a sense of your inner critic, give it an appropriate name so you can call it out—and laugh at it—when you recognize it. For example: "I realize you're nervous about the client presentation, Sir Harps-a-Lot. But you're making me unnecessarily anxious. I'll do a much better job if you'd kindly leave me to it."

Often, our inner critics raise or highlight false beliefs. The more these negative statements get repeated, the more we tend to believe them, deep down. Whenever we do notice these negative statements, it is important to recognize them as false and to dispute them.

In Chapter 6, you had the opportunity to challenge unhelpful beliefs. Apply those techniques to recognize and manage your inner critic.

For example, if your inner critic is saying "I'm too old to make it as a saxophone player", the first step is to realize that this is not objectively true. This is a false belief.

Step two is to contest it. Generate as much evidence to the contrary as you can. (E.g., *I know several successful saxophone players who recorded their first album when they were much older than me. I'm a better player now than I was ten years ago. It's only too late if I give up now.*)

Step three is to replace it with a more helpful belief. For example: *I am becoming a successful saxophone player.*

Now, write down everything you can think of to support this preferred belief. (E.g., *I'm a good musician; I book regular gigs; I've received praise from professionals I admire; I know I'm better than that group I heard at Jazz Fest. If they made an album, so can I.*) Make a compelling case for any belief that will support you in your endeavor.

TECHNIQUE

Manage Your Inner Critic

---

1. What kinds of things does your inner critic tend to say?
2. What tone does your inner critic use?
3. Who does your inner critic sound like?
4. What is your inner critic afraid of?
5. Name your inner critic so you can call it out—and laugh at it—when you hear it.

   Henceforth, I shall call my inner critic _____________.
6. What false beliefs does your inner critic raise? Make a list.
7. Take each false belief, one at a time. For each, ask yourself:

   - What evidence is there to the contrary? What is the real truth here? What is the objective reality? Write out as many refutations as you can.
   - List alternative beliefs you'd prefer.
   - Write down everything you can think of that supports your preferred beliefs. Be compelling!

Next, consider how you might become a better friend to yourself, going forward.

Stop for a moment and think about your best friend. What are they like? How do they treat you, on a daily basis? How have they helped you during difficult times? What have they done or said that demonstrates their friendship and affection for you? How have they supported or appreciated your talents?

We can learn a lot from our friends. Our true friends support us, encourage us, and help us problem solve. They reassure us that we are okay, our ideas are sound, our projects are worthwhile, and our talents are considerable. They help us through difficult times and help us celebrate our accomplishments.

How could you do the same for yourself?

ACTIVITY

1. Find a photo of your best friend. Keep it in front of you as you answer the following:
   - What does my best friend think are my best qualities?
   - What key messages would my best friend want me to know about myself?
   - What does my best friend encourage me to do more of?
   - What does my best friend encourage me to do less of?
2. This week, practice being your own best friend. Treat yourself nicely. If you find yourself speaking harshly to yourself, stop and reframe your words to be kinder. If it's helpful, imagine what your best friend would say in a given situation. Hear their voice in your mind.

BONUS ACTIVITY

1. Write yourself a letter of encouragement. Include:
   - The key messages your best friend would likely say.
   - The key messages that you know would be helpful for you at this time.
   - The things you would like to believe.
2. Keep your letter somewhere where you can retrieve it and read it when you need a boost.

◆

RECOGNIZE AND UTILIZE YOUR STRENGTHS

Do you tend to gloss over your accomplishments? If so, pause for a moment to remind yourself of what you have achieved so far. (Please do the following activity before reading ahead.)

ACTIVITY

List at least ten things you've accomplished or achieved. This might include:

- Things you've done that you are proud of.
- Goals you've reached.
- Challenges you've overcome.
- Problems you've solved.
- Things you've created.
- Successful relationships (personal and professional).
- Prizes, awards, badges, certificates, diplomas, degrees, credentials, etc.
- Key life milestones (e.g., acquiring jobs, homes).
- Things you've learned.

You have already accomplished a lot in your life. You have achieved goals. You have solved problems. You have overcome challenges. Bask in that for a moment.

Next, give yourself some credit. Consider your inner strengths. Think about the qualities and skills that you used to accomplish everything on your previous list.

Go deeper. What do you appreciate about yourself? What do you like best about yourself? What do you love about yourself?

KEY QUESTIONS

1. What are your strong points?
2. What are your talents?
3. What are your skills?
4. What is as easy as breathing for you?
5. What came easily to you when you were a child?
6. For what abilities do you receive the most compliments?
7. What is your "superpower"?
8. What do you like best about yourself? This might include:
    - Aspects of your personality
    - Things about yourself that make you happy
    - Your values

Once you remind yourself of your strengths, the next question is this: to what extent are you utilizing them in your current life?

For example, if you are sociable and socialize easily, to what extent are you using this strength to accomplish your desired goals? Are you involving others in your efforts? Are you networking?

If you are utilizing all your strengths, great! Most of us, however, are not deploying all our talents to the extent we could. It is helpful to take stock and identify any skills that are currently underutilized.

When you do, you can detect new opportunities. If, for example, you know you are an adventurer deep down, but you realize that you are not being very adventurous these days, you can ask why you are not utilizing this strength. Perhaps you are tired. Maybe you are avoiding taking new risks due to fear of repeating past regrets or disappointments. What is curtailing your use of this strength?

Give some thought as to how you might utilize this strength, going forward. For example, how you might be more adventurous in your current life? What tiny risks could you take this week?

ACTIVITY

To what extent are you utilizing your strengths?

Go through the list you made in answering the previous set of questions. Put a checkmark beside those qualities that are being fully utilized in your current life.

Circle anything that is less evident in your current life.

Next, focus on each circled item, one at a time. Ask yourself:

- Why am I not utilizing this strength?
- How might I utilize this strength more in my current life?
- What small steps can I take to utilize this strength more this week?

◆

ACCENTUATE THE POSITIVE

If you have been focused on unwanted events in your past, you have been giving attention to negative things.

It can become a deeply ingrained pattern to focus more on what you don't want, rather than what you do. Or to focus on what's wrong, rather than what is working well in your life.

Right now, you can decide to operate differently. You can focus on what you **do** want, rather than what you don't. You can give your attention to what **is** working well in your life, rather than what isn't.

ACTIVITY

1. What is working well in your life? Make a list.
2. Keep your list handy where you will see it regularly (e.g., on your computer, in your phone or wallet).
3. When you notice negative thoughts in your head, re-read your list.

Going forward, be purposeful. When you catch yourself dwelling on negative things, pause and pivot. Look for anything good in your life. Seek any more positive thoughts.

For example, if you find yourself thinking, "*This will never work*", that can feel awful. Pause and search for any truthful thought that feels better. Identify any idea that gives you even a tiny bit of relief. Consider any of the following:

It's too early to tell if this will work or not. I need to suspend judgment.

This might work.

I know I can find a way to make this work.

Do any of these alternatives seem truthful and make you feel better? If so, great, use that. If not, keep brainstorming until you find a thought that does.

TECHNIQUE
Reframe Negative Thoughts

---

1. Write out the negative thought.
2. Brainstorm alternatives until you find a different thought that seems truthful and makes you feel better.

Another way to accentuate the positive is to keep track of what **is** getting done, rather than what **isn't**. Acknowledge your accomplishments, big and small, every day.

At the end of the day, take a moment to write down all you got done. Give yourself credit (literally) for everything you did. Include major accomplishments and minor triumphs. Julia Cameron (author of *The Artist's Way*) calls this her 'Ta Dah' list. For example, *I brushed my teeth, I made that call, I started that report, I cleaned the sink, I meditated, I read five pages, I made a tasty lunch, etc.*

I love this practice because it shifts focus from your 'To Do's" to your "Ta Dah's".

TECHNIQUE

Nightly "Ta Dah" List

At the end of the day, take a few minutes to write a list of everything you accomplished, big and small.

Another simple end-of-day ritual is to scan your day for "the best thing that happened today". As you are preparing for sleep, remind yourself of the day's highlights. Identify one (or more) good things you experienced. This should feel positive and gratifying—and is much more pleasant than, say, dwelling over something you "should" have done or didn't do. Or fretting about tomorrow's tasks.

When you can end your day on a positive note, you tee up a better night's sleep and a pleasant start on the following morning.

TECHNIQUE

"Today's Highlights"

When you are ready to sleep, think back over your day. Identify the best things you experienced. Take a moment to savor them.

◆

CHOOSE YOUR PATH FORWARD

At this point in your life, what do you want? What is important to you? How do you want to operate?

Imagine that you could press a reset button and start your life fresh. Guess what? You can. You can purposefully decide how you would like to live, from here on.

ACTIVITY

1. Write down as many responses as you can to the following questions:
   - How do I want to live my life?
   - What do I want to do more of?
   - What do I want to do less of?
   - What kind of person do I want to be? How do I want to operate?
   - What makes me happy?
   - How can I live a happier, healthier life?
2. Brainstorm a list of small actions you could take this week to do more of what you love and less of what you don't.
3. Make a point of taking at least one of these actions this week.
4. Make a recurring weekly appointment with yourself to read your responses to question 1. Each week, make a point of doing at least one thing towards living your preferred life.

Once you have given some thought to how you want to be living your life, consider your path forward. Where would you like to go from here? What would you like to do, experience, explore, learn, accomplish, acquire or complete?

ACTIVITY

Brainstorm answers to the following questions:

- What would you like to do, experience, explore, learn, accomplish, acquire, or complete in your **personal life**?
- What would you like to do, experience, explore, learn, accomplish, acquire, or complete in your **work life**?
- Consider your **Life Dreams**. What would you like to do, experience, explore, learn, accomplish, acquire, or complete?

Give some extra attention to your Life Dreams. If you have been brooding over a past regret or disappointment, did it involve an important dream—one that had been hindered, deferred, or thwarted?

Ask yourself: is this a dream or goal to which you still aspire today? If so, how can you take steps towards achieving that dream, starting now? What lessons can you apply from the past to enhance your success going forward? What alternatives are there for proceeding? What could you try doing a different way? What completely new approach could you try?

If you are concerned that you've missed your chance to achieve your dream, let me reassure you: it is never too late. If this dream is still important to you, it is worth pursuing. You'll get more joy and fulfillment from working towards your dream than by giving up.

Julia Child was almost forty when she learned to cook and found her true passion. It took another decade for her to publish her classic cookbook and she didn't start her seminal TV show until she was fifty-one.

Laura Ingalls Wilder began writing a newspaper column in her forties. She didn't write or publish her *Little House* series until she was in her sixties.

Peter Mark Roget didn't start compiling his *Thesaurus of English Words and Phrases* until he was seventy. It was first published when he was seventy-three.

Grandma Moses began painting when she was seventy-six. She created more than a thousand paintings over the next twenty-five years.

Betty Reid Soskin began her career as a park ranger in the US National Park Service at eighty-five because she felt compelled to share what she and other Black women had experienced during World War II. She earned honors and accolades and was conferred with the Lifetime Achievement Award at the 2018 Glamour Awards hosted by *Glamour* magazine. She didn't retire until she was 100.

If it is still important to you, persist. Consider, for example, when film critic Roger Ebert won the fabled *New Yorker* Cartoon Caption Contest. "So, what," you may think. "He was a smart guy. A Pulitzer Prize winning journalist. Big deal." What's interesting about it is that he failed in his first 106 attempts. It wasn't until his 107th entry that he finally won. And it wasn't as if Roger Ebert didn't have other things going on. He was a multitasking syndicated columnist and blogger who hosted an annual film festival and wrote books. He published a cookbook, for heaven's sake, even though he was physically unable to eat. Actually, that's another awesome display of persistence: when Roger Ebert's cancer robbed him of the capacity to eat solid food he went ahead and wrote the cookbook he'd always wanted to produce.

Know that "not following their dreams" is one of the three top regrets hospice chaplain Tenzin Kiyosaki hears from patients who have less than six months to live. If something is important to you, persist.

ACTIVITY

1. Think of an instance in which you persisted.
   - What was the experience like for you at the time?
   - How did you continue on?
   - What were the benefits of persisting?
2. How can you apply these insights to your Life Dream? What actions can you take to move forward?

If, however, your dream is less attractive to you now, then give yourself permission to stop mourning what didn't happen. It could well be that you didn't *really* want what you thought you did. It could be that your earlier goal was something you (or someone close to you) believed you "should" do, rather than a true passion. For example, maybe you didn't get into medical school...and maybe that's a good thing. Maybe the blood and gore and educational costs and long hours and constant threat of lawsuits just aren't that appealing to you, if you're honest about it.

Or it could be that you weren't (and aren't) willing to put in the effort required to make your dream come true. Maybe it's more of a fantasy than a life goal. *Sure, I'd love to be a size zero... but I'm not prepared to undertake the chronic starvation, oppressive exercise schedule, and probable surgery required to achieve that particular physique. Nor do I want to be miserable or stressed out or unpleasant to be around. Really, I'd rather eat foods I love and accept having a wider waist.*

ACTIVITY

1. Write down a list of your major Life Dreams.
2. Review your list. If you were being honest with yourself, which of these are your real, true, fervent desires? Which would you most like to have happen, going forward? Circle them. Which are not? Cross them off your list.

In this section you have generated options for proceeding. What is most interesting, exciting, and important to you now? What makes your heart sing? Choose your top priorities.

ACTIVITY

1. Reread your answers to the activities in this section.
2. Choose one to three things you really, truly want to do. What are your current top priorities?

Once you have chosen your current priorities, chart a course of action to move forward. Any little act you take will feel better than brooding about past regrets or disappointments. Every step you take toward your current priority takes you farther away from your past.

Begin by focusing on your top priority. Use the following steps to devise an implementation plan.

TECHNIQUE

Devise An Implementation Plan

- Describe your priority. What you want to do, experience, explore, learn, accomplish, acquire, or complete? *Be as detailed as possible.*
- Deep down, why is this important to you? What is your true motivation? If you could make this happen, what would it mean to you?
- How can you make it happen? What needs to occur? By when?
- What schedule is reasonable and doable for you?
- What are the smallest next steps you can take?
- What is already in place to help you make it happen? What support do you have?
- What information do you need?
- What resources do you require? How might you acquire them?
- What potential obstacles and challenges might arise that would interfere? *Include how you might get in your own way.*
- Brainstorm at least three ways you could counter or address each potential obstacle or challenge.

ACTIVITY

Review your answers in this section. Choose (at least) one action you can do this week. Make a point of doing it.

◆

MANAGE EXPECTATIONS

As you move forward, be aware of how you are thinking and feeling about what you are doing.

What energy are you bringing to your efforts? Are you content, happy, or excited? Are you anxious or worried? Whatever you are feeling will influence how things unfold for you.

To the extent that you derive joy and fulfillment from the process, you are more likely to succeed. (And if you're not enjoying the process, why are you doing this, anyway?)

But some days will be better than others. On those occasions when you don't feel good about what you are doing, pause and look for any thought that feels better. Remind yourself why you have chosen this path. What benefits can you glean along the way? What learning or other opportunities are there?

Are your expectations reasonable? Do you tend to be overly optimistic or unnecessarily negative about what you are doing?

How can you temper your hopes or fears? Aim for a baseline balance of "motivating" and "realistic"—while leaving the door open for happy surprises and successes along the way.

Also, release expectations about how, exactly, things "should" unfold. Many paths can lead to your goals...to the extent that you allow them. If you are overly insistent on things happening in one particular way, you may be setting yourself up for heartbreak. Yes, you want an agent to sign you...and there are a thousand ways that can happen. It doesn't help if you lock onto one and only one path to get there.

How can you stay motivated as you move forward? How can you monitor your progress so that you can appreciate it? How can you recognize and reward any forward movement?

For example, if you are trying to write a book, you could keep track of the number of words or pages you write each day, or the amount of time you spend on your project. It can be gratifying to watch those numbers add up.

What will work for you? How can you monitor your progress in your desired endeavor?

Find ways to focus on the process, rather than discounting anything that isn't your desired end point or product. How can you enjoy your progress along the way?

You have little control over much in the world...except for your own actions and attitudes. Much as you might like to, you cannot control others' reactions or decisions. You can't control global events or trends. All you can do is to keep taking steps to advance your own work—regardless of what's happening around you. Make any needed adjustments and keep moving forward.

If you find yourself overwhelmed or stressed, prioritize. Rather than listing EVERYTHING you have to do, for example, focus on the one or two most important things you'd like to accomplish at this point in time. Ask yourself: what is my top priority today? Concentrate on that first.

When you've given that sufficient attention, if you want to do more you can then ask, "What's the next most important thing I need to do today?"

If you get stuck, simplify. Ask, "What is the easiest way to move forward? What is my easiest option at this point?" Focus on small steps forward in your desired direction. A journey of a thousand miles begins with a single step. Think of each step forward as a win.

KEY QUESTIONS

---

1. How do you feel about the path you've chosen? Are any adjustments needed?
2. What are your expectations? To what extent are they overly optimistic or unnecessarily pessimistic? What adjustments are needed?
3. How can you monitor and reward your progress?
4. What can you put in place to keep you on track and moving forward?

◆

DEAL MORE EFFECTIVELY WITH FUTURE REGRETS AND DISAPPOINTMENTS

Sorry, but you are likely to encounter some regrets, disappointments, and "mistakes" in the future. Everyone does.

It's natural to be upset or to mourn when unwanted things happen. But after you express your reaction, then what?

Hopefully, you will utilize the tools and techniques in this book to help you process what happened, assess your options for moving forward, and then proceed accordingly. When unwanted things occur:

- Examine what happened (Chapter 4)
- Seek silver linings (Chapter 5)
- Tell a different story (Chapter 6)

- Forgive yourself and others (Chapter 7)
- Take action (Chapter 8)
- Let it go (Chapter 9), and,
- Move forward (Chapter 10)

Acknowledgements

Thank you to everyone who shared their stories. It's not easy to reveal regrets, disappointments, or past "mistakes" and I hope that doing so helps your healing. Your examples certainly are helping others.

Sincere thanks to Janna Stewart and Glenna Quinn Felsman for reading earlier drafts of this book. Your feedback and suggestions for improvement are most appreciated.

In gratitude for many blessings, a portion of the proceeds of this book is being donated to charity.